CHANGING FORTUNES

After personal and professional disaster in America, Crystal Tempest, a qualified surveyor, had returned to England to rebuild her life. Her uncle, the managing director of a large construction company, agreed to employ her on condition that she worked on a building site for six months, telling nobody that she was his niece. Crystal was happy with this arrangement, but when she came up against the arrogant architect Dan Farraday it seemed that fate hadn't quite finished playing games with her . . .

Books by Joyce Johnson
in the Linford Romance Library:

JOYCE JOHNSON

CHANGING FORTUNES

Complete and Unabridged

LINFORD
Leicester

First published in Great Britain in 1996

First Linford Edition
published 2001

Copyright © 1996 by Joyce Johnson
All rights reserved

British Library CIP Data

Johnson, Joyce, *1931* –
  Changing fortunes.—Large print ed.—
Linford romance library
1. Love stories
2. Large type books
I. Title
813.5′4 [F]

ISBN 0–7089–9725–2

Published by
F. A. Thorpe (Publishing)
Anstey, Leicestershire

Set by Words & Graphics Ltd.
Anstey, Leicestershire
Printed and bound in Great Britain by
T. J. International Ltd., Padstow, Cornwall

This book is printed on acid-free paper

1

'No! No, and no again! Crystal, don't you know me by now? Once my mind's made up, that's it! I've told you before! No more family in the business. If it's money you want . . . '

'No!'

It was Crystal's turn to snap the negative, but her beautiful, wide dark-eyed smile tempered with warmth as she moved to perch on the arm of Richard Drummond's leather swivel chair. Almost before she could walk, she'd been able to wheedle her way with Uncle Dick, but this time it was for something much more important than the sweeties, or extra pocket money, of her childhood. Crystal Tempest was desperate.

'A loan then?' Dick suggested.

He knew the power of his niece's eyes. They were just like his sister

Helen's. Crystal put an arm around his shoulders.

'Not even a loan. I don't want money. Mum and Dad would never forgive me. You've been so generous to us always.'

She dropped a kiss on the top of his forehead, leaned over, and flicked out a paper from the top of his 'In'-tray.

'You know what I want. It's no good pretending you haven't read my letter.'

She thrust it under his nose.

'Here — my c.v., and application to join Drummond Construction Limited. I'm as well qualified as most. I've had experience in this country, and two years in the States. They don't discriminate against women surveyors there. And, legally, you can't . . . '

Dick Drummond, founder and managing director of one of the largest construction companies in Europe, was unaccustomed to argument, especially in his own office. Ruthless single-mindedness and total dedication had put Drummond's at the top of the tree, and that's where he aimed to keep it, whatever the problems. That being so, surely he could cope with those pleading eyes? He cleared his throat.

'Crystal, it's not because you're a woman, you must know that, and I'm sure you're first rate at your job. I recognise your qualifications, and your references are excellent, but you know well enough why I can't employ you, so don't play the innocent. It's below the belt.'

Crystal stood up. She was loose-limbed, tall and slim, with long dark-blonde hair. Dick marvelled again at the likeness to his much-loved younger sister. He softened his refusal with a smile.

'It's just because you are Crystal Tempest that I can't give you the job. You're Helen's child — my niece — a Drummond!'

'All the more reason . . .'

His fist crashed down on the mahogany desk top.

'Wrong. That is just the reason. Look

what happened to your father.'

'Oh, Uncle Dick, that was twenty years ago. He doesn't hold you responsible, nor does Mum. They're happy, in Spain, at your villa . . . '

'Jack's a cripple. You never knew him as a young man, full of energy. Drummond's as good as killed him, and I'm Drummond's!'

Crystal impatiently shook back her hair.

'That's just melodrama, an excuse. I'm not going to have an accident, and what about Neville? He's your son. You employ him.'

'That was a very big mistake, another reason not to employ family at Drummond's. It doesn't work, Crystal, and that's that.'

'It's so unfair! If I'd sent my letter under another name, at least, you'd have given me an interview.'

He scanned it briefly, though he knew it by heart already, and looked her in the eye.

'Yes, yes. Probably.'

4

'Well then?'

He sighed.

'Why Drummond's, Crystal? There's a score of firms out there.'

But he knew the answer. Crystal stuck her hands into the pockets of her corded jeans.

'Uncle Dick, don't you think I've tried? Why do you think I've finally swallowed my pride and grovelled — still am grovelling, you may have noticed? I've been everywhere. Recession, hard times in the industry, quite a lot of thinly disguised male chauvinism — it's all against me.

'Maybe I should never have gone to the States. I had a foot on the ladder here at Broomhill's, but they're not taking anyone on at the moment. I'm getting desperate. It's not just the money. I really need to work. I've been unemployed for six months. It's no joke, I can tell you. You just can't imagine.'

She gave him a lopsided grin and that did it! Dick Drummond, merciless tycoon, with a reputation for being tougher than reinforced concrete, felt his resolve turning to putty. The very first time he'd seen that grin, she'd been toothless! He put his head in his hands.

He stayed there so long, Crystal took pity on him. She picked up her bag and took a tentative step towards him.

'Uncle, it's OK. Forget I asked. You're right, it's not fair of me. Something'll turn up. I'll just keep on trying. How about dinner one night, just you, me and Neville?'

Her uncle looked up, giving her a steely glance.

'I'd rather not socialise with my son at present, but I'll accept your invitation.' He changed the subject abruptly. 'Tell me, why did you leave America when you did? According to your mother, it was all just too wonderful for words out there.'

Crystal's generous mouth tightened.

'Personal,' she said and then clammed up.

Her brain screamed danger. She was trying to blank out what had happened in Nevada.

That was all Dick was getting, and he knew it. He recognised, and respected, the Drummond stubbornness. He also knew when he was beaten.

'Right, Ms Tempest, here's the deal. You win. I'll take you on at Drummond's but — hey, hey!'

He fended off her ecstatic hug.

'You haven't heard the terms yet. Hmph! Looks as though you'll need to do some work here, too.' He circled her biceps with finger and thumb.

'Tut, tut, girl, you've gone all flabby!'

Crystal pulled away quickly. He was right, though. Ever since she'd left America, she'd allowed herself to get out of condition, put on too much weight. There'd been too much comfort eating, too much sitting around watching television, trying to forget . . .

'I don't mean to be personal. I'll explain. Here are my terms of employment. First, nobody must know you're my niece. We've different names, and you've been out of England for well over two years, so that's no problem.'

'Neville will know.'

'He won't be working anywhere near you. And I'll put him in the picture.'

He looked grim, and Crystal said hastily, 'Fine by me. All the better, in fact. Second?'

'Second, you start at the bottom, like all my professional staff. You'll be on site, manual labour, six months hard! And I mean hard! No gender concessions.'

'None asked for, nor expected. You do know I did all that in the States a couple of years ago? Six months in Arizona, in the summer, in the desert!'

'So where you're going'll be a piece of cake.'

'I'm happy to do it over again, anywhere you send me.'

Crystal had grown up alongside Drummond's growth, and she'd done her homework on its present position. Her uncle's success was, in the main part, due to having several irons in several fires. Drummond Construction networked Great Britain and was putting tentacles into Europe and beyond.

'You can start a month from now.'

'A month! Why not straight away?'

'Because, dear niece, from the look of you, if you'll excuse the liberty, you wouldn't last five minutes with a shovel in your hands, as you are at present. You're simply not fit enough. I don't know what happened to you across the Atlantic, and I can see you aren't going to tell me, but it doesn't seem to have done you a lot of good.'

He ripped off a counterfoil from the book he'd been writing on and held out a cheque.

'No, I don't want any more argument, or the deal's off. This is made out to Gentleman Jim's Gym — ridiculous name, first-class business. Jim'll fix things for you — tone you up, and thin you down. And lay off the chocolates. I know you of old, and as a fellow chocoholic, I can sympathise.'

His face softened.

'Aw, don't look at me like that, Chrissie. I feel a heel. I've been a brute. Why don't you forget the whole thing? We'll have a slap-up dinner, chocolates included, and think of something else for you to do. I'll see if I can pull a few strings.'

'Absolutely not.'

Crystal took the cheque, gasped at the amount, hesitated, then folded it up and put it in her jeans' pocket.

'Thanks. You'll have this back within the year, and I shan't need a month. A couple of weeks'll do.'

She kissed his cheek affectionately.

'You're a darling. You always were my favourite relative. I won't let you down, you'll see.'

She gave a casual wave and was gone, leaving Drummond's managing director curiously flat.

Before he resumed his normal business of the day, Richard Drummond red-ringed the date on his desk diary — one month from today's date. In his crowded schedule, he squeezed in the word Crystal, followed by a large question mark. For once, the tycoon wondered if he'd done the right thing, then slapped the diary shut. He had plenty more serious things to worry about at present.

He loved his niece, and truly he was delighted to help her. Whatever had happened in the States had obviously knocked her for six, but Crystal was a survivor. Drummond's survival was another matter, and needed all his attention right now. Dismissing family from his mind, he picked up the phone. There was a lot of work to do — and not too much time.

Nearly six months later, Crystal was up to her ankles in mud, working in the teeth of a vicious, winter gale. Rain streamed off her yellow oilskins and drummed on to her hard hat, as she barrowed debris across the bleak building site. But she was happy — for the first time since she'd left Nevada

11

twelve months earlier.

Her muscles ached, in spite of her three weeks intensive work in Jim's Gym, and her subsequent months of back-breaking labour on site, but she whistled softly to herself as she slipped and slithered along.

In spite of his tough words, Richard Drummond had wisely selected a fairly easy option for his niece's six months hard labour. His firm had won a contract to build a by-pass round a market town some fifty miles outside London. On a new site, with a new crew, Crystal started with an even chance.

Her experiences in the States had prepared her for a certain amount of male chauvinism. She'd learned on site out there to adopt a tough-cookie role, but intended to play a more fined-down version for the UK market!

Pity she hadn't kept up the tough-gal approach with Dwight in California, she couldn't help thinking bitterly. She tried so hard not to think of that time, and work was helping as she'd known it would.

In the event, it wasn't necessary to act tough on the Drayton site. She met little opposition. The automatic male banter was easy to deal with and the crew had accepted her from the beginning. Once she'd demonstrated her willingness to tackle any job the foreman threw at her, she earned respect as well.

Crystal was a qualified surveyor, with an appreciation of the practicalities of her job, and hard, physical labour was what she needed at this low point in her life. Up at dawn for the journey to the site, back home in the dark, she was too healthily tired to do little more than cook supper and tumble into bed. It suited her down to the ground, and she wasn't thinking beyond her six month's trial.

She was too encased in protective clothing to see her watch, but her body-clock told her it was tea-break time. She headed for the workers' cabin. There was no-one else in the stuffy room where they brewed up, and she wondered whether she'd misjudged the time. She took off her hat and eased her hair, severely tied back in a long pony tail, out of her wet collar.

Through the steamed-up window, she saw Bob, the foreman, head bent against the driving rain, coming towards the building. He opened the door, bringing the stinging wind inside.

'Crystal! Just the woman I need. Pete's rung. He needs a spare whacker. Can you run it over? He's at the other end of the site. Donovan's loading it on to the bucket now. Won't take you long.'

'Sure.'

Crystal tucked her hair back inside her collar, put on her hat and went outside again. She jumped at any chance to drive the huge trucks, much more fun than shifting debris. The whacker, a heavy, concrete column used for compacting drainage trenches, was already in the bucket of the huge digger set high, so as not to block the driver's view.

She acknowledged Donovan's effort with a wave, climbed up into the seat of the cab, put on ear muffs, and switched into gear. She peered through the windscreen, but all she could see was mud and churned-up earth. A rough dirt road had been marked out across the site, and Crystal slewed the truck on to it.

Huge, concrete pipes were piled by the track. It was rougher at this end, and large pot-holes pitted the earth. Conscious of the weight in the swinging bucket above her, she slowed down, just as she saw the streak of red coming straight for her. She couldn't believe it. What idiot would be driving at that speed over such rough ground? She hit the brakes hard, skidded into a deep rut, felt the bucket bounce high, and saw the whacker begin to tip over!

'Look out!' she yelled, as the car, instead of stopping, sped across the front of her huge vehicle.

Crystal closed her eyes, clutching her ear muffs, but felt the reverberations as the concrete column crashed squarely on to the car, before bouncing to the ground. Fearfully, she opened her eyes, then gasped with relief. The car had a long boot, which had taken the brunt of the blow. It had lost its sleek, sporty look, but the occupant must be unharmed — apart from the shock.

Crystal swung down from the cab. The stupid idiot could easily have been killed, and although it was the driver's own fault, she'd have felt responsible. A cold knot coiled in her stomach, as she thought of her uncle's reaction.

The car's occupant was already out of the car. She registered him as tall, broad-shouldered, long-legged, muscular — all clad in a very expensive suit, which was already several shades darkened by the rain. The streaming wet didn't seem to deter him, as he strode towards her. Even through the murky day, she saw the blazing blue fury of his eyes.

'You . . . ' she started to say, but he got there first.

'What in heaven's name do you think you're doing? This is a roadworks site, not a racing circuit. You were travelling at a criminal speed, and if you loaded that thing yourself, you deserve to be shot. It was bound to tip out at the first opportunity, and you were giving it plenty. I watched you, driving like a maniac! You could have killed me.'

Pity I didn't, ran through Crystal's head, as she tried to interrupt the man's thunderous fury. Behind him, she saw a yellow site van coming towards them. It skidded to a halt, and Pete, the under foreman, leaped out. The man swung round to include Pete in his tirade.

'If you're the foreman, I want this — this imbecile off the site, and out of a job, as of right now. You can see what his idiotic recklessness has done.'

He moved aside to indicate the mangled boot of his car, and the sight added fuel to the already leaping flames of his temper.

'Do you hear me? I want this man sacked. Now!'

Crystal opened her mouth, her own burning anger rising to meet his, but Pete put a hand on her arm.

'Just a sec!'

He turned up his collar, as a fresh blast of rain swept across the mud. Crystal felt she was trapped in a bizarre nightmare, and part of that nightmare was her loss of speech. Choked by anger and injustice, she struggled to say something.

'Don't say a thing just yet,' Pete warned her. 'Let me handle it. I want to know who he is first. Don't worry, you'll get your chance.'

The man came over to them, glowering impatience.

'What are you waiting for? I want to see him go, right now, and preferably on foot. You realise this man could have killed me?'

Crystal had had enough. It was all very well for Pete. He wasn't being wiped out.

18

'I . . . ' she began.

Again, Pete tried to shut her up. He addressed the stranger.

'Who are you, and what's your business on this site?'

'Dan Farraday,' he spat out. 'Now, this man's name. I'll deal with him if you can't, or won't.'

Crystal and Pete spoke simultaneously.

'She's not . . . '

'My name's Crystal Tempest. I know you've had a shock, but I object to your attitude and manner most strongly. You're a rude, arrogant bully.'

She drew herself up tall, facing him head on with proud belligerence.

'OK, Pete, I'm not admitting a thing, but he was the maniac, driving straight for me. How anyone could miss seeing a huge yellow JCB out in this wasteland is beyond belief. You must have been in a dream — drunk, maybe?'

She was pleased with the astonished look of shock that had temporarily replaced the black anger on the man's face.

'Bob Merton's my boss,' she went on. 'He's at the site office, and I'm more than happy to go along and explain what happened. I don't have to take orders from you, Mr Farraday, whoever you are, nor do I have to take any more misplaced abuse. Pete, I'll take the truck back.'

She turned on her heel, and went to climb back into the cab, but found her arm caught in a tight grip, and her body whirled round to face Dan Farraday.

'No, you don't. You'll come with me. You're responsible for the damage done to my car. You're not skulking off, nor getting to your foreman first, fluttering your eyes at him.'

Crystal gasped. His face was thrust close to hers, and she felt a jolt of misgiving. His eyes were cobalt hard, and his mouth, which she imagined could be softly sensuous, was taut with rage. Crystal's nerve wavered. He should have looked ridiculous, water streaming off him, practically soaked to the skin, but somehow it enhanced the primitive power surging round him. She felt that power, too, in the grip on her arm.

'Let me go. I'm not skulking off. Pete?' she appealed, but he was looking distinctly embarrassed.

'Er — Mr Farraday, Crystal won't run off. The JCB needs to go back. I'll see to your car, then take you over to the office.'

'It may still be driveable, but no thanks to her. And she comes with me.'

'Did you want to see Bob Merton?' Pete's tone was placatory, and Crystal squirmed, trying to pull free.

'No, but I do now. The last thing I expected here was an idiot woman driver let loose with heavy equipment. What's Merton thinking of? Aren't there enough good men unemployed? Does Dick Drummond know about it, and if he does, is he going senile?'

Crystal jerked herself free.

'Don't you dare . . . ' then she shut her mouth.

She couldn't defend her uncle. She wasn't even supposed to know him, but she could send this odious man a withering glance of contempt. Impervious to rain or scorn, he returned it with a black scowl. Pete shifted uneasily.

'You're soaked, Mr Farraday. I've got spare oilskins in the van.'

'No, thanks.' He moved towards his car. 'I'll take her back now. I'll have her off this site if it's the last thing I do.'

'Let's hope it is then,' Crystal muttered, and to Pete, she said, 'Can't I take the truck back on my own? Do I have go to with him?'

'He's Dan Farraday,' Pete hissed, as the man got into his damaged car and started the engine.

'So?'

'Haven't you heard of Farraday and Winch, the architects?'

'Farraday — didn't he — they — win a big design prize in Italy fairly recently?'

'That's them. Dan Farraday's one of the best brains in the design construction business.'

'What — roadworks?'

'Not usually. More domestic — town centres — leisure complexes — that sort of thing.'

'What's he doing here then?'

'No idea, but you couldn't have picked a worse person to tangle with. He's a pretty rich and powerful bloke. At least his car's working, though he's probably got half a dozen Porsches like that at home.'

'Come on. Get in,' Dan Farraday said impatiently from inside the car.

Crystal took a deep breath.

'Sorry, Pete. I'll square it with Bob. He can try to get me sacked if he wants to, but I'm not going anywhere with the brute.'

She climbed into the cab and quickly reversed the JCB away from the car. It gave her a deal of satisfaction to see the expression on Dan Farraday's face. He got out, leaving the engine running, and strode towards her.

'Didn't you understand? I said come with me.'

Crystal smiled, pointing to her ear muffs.

'Can't hear you,' she mouthed.

His eyes blazed, held hers for a long moment, then he said slowly and deliberately, so there was no doubt she would understand, ear muffs or not.

'All right, Miss Tempest. If that's the way you want to play it!'

She watched him in the driving mirror as he went back to his car, and the set of his body told her that, although she may have won a minor point, he hadn't finished with her by any means.

Seconds later, the red car, with its badly damaged boot, shot past, heading in the direction of the main office. Much more slowly, and with deep misgiving, she followed in the JCB, her euphoric earlier mood quite evaporated.

2

Crystal didn't hurry along, delaying her arrival back at the site headquarters for as long as possible. Her encounter with Dan Farraday had shaken her. She hated his attitude, but there was something more. A nervous tension twanged her nerve ends far more than the normal upsetting accident warranted.

Back in Nevada last year, her entanglement with Dwight Rogers had been disastrous, both professionally and emotionally. The incident with Dan Farraday brought it all rushing back. She had badly misjudged Dwight's character and intentions, and the awful train of events set in motion by her lack of judgment would haunt her till she died.

Even now, back in England, the aftermath of those events could still reach out and pull her back. She shuddered. The rebuilding of her life, starting at the bottom again at Drummond's, was in process, and Crystal's spirited nature, and resilience, were helping. It had all been going so well, until this awful man in the sports car had come bowling across the landscape.

The cluster of cabins was close now, and there was the red Porsche, parked outside Bob Merton's office. He was still there, as she'd known he would be. She allowed a moment of honest reflection. Had she been driving too fast? Could it have been her fault? His furious, unreasonable behaviour had blurred her recollection, but more importantly, it might cost her her job.

No-one knew she was Dick Drummond's niece, and she couldn't and wouldn't capitalise on that. Neither did anyone know, nor would they care, that she was a professional — a well-qualified surveyor. To her workmates, and to Bob Merton, she was simply an expendable body, and there would be plenty more queuing up to take her place.

Crystal had a locker in the cabin adjoining the foreman's office. As she went in, to get rid of her outer gear, Dan Farraday opened the door from Bob Merton's office. His face was grim, but he'd replaced his sodden shirt and jacket with a casual, crew-neck sweater. Dark hair, rapidly drying out, sprang away from his head in strong thick waves.

Crystal did her best to pretend he wasn't there, but it was difficult. He seemed to fill the doorway. She could just see Bob in the office beyond, on the telephone, with his back to her. She shrugged off her waterproof jacket and removed her hard hat, pulling out her thick pony tail.

Dan's blue eyes narrowed.

'You took your time,' he said curtly. 'I'm late for an appointment.'

'I didn't want to break the speed limit, and I'm sure you don't need me here. You've decided I'm to blame, and

27

no doubt your version of what happened will carry more weight than mine, even if mine is the truth.'

The wintry weather had prematurely darkened the day, and there was very little daylight left. The men would be coming in soon at the end of their shift, preparing to return to London. There was no-one else in the hut except the two of them. It was stuffy, the windows were steamed up, and the gas heater, hissing in the corner, threw out an oppressive heat.

Crystal could hear Bob Merton on the phone, probably ordering her replacement, she thought, with a baleful glance at Dan Farraday. Why didn't he go, instead of standing there, surveying her with that superior expression?

Opening the locker, she took out dry socks and leggings, and pulled off her waterproof trousers. Dan Farraday continued to watch her. She glared at him.

'Do you mind? I want to change my leggings.'

'Go ahead. I presume Drummond's haven't gone as far as providing you with private changing facilities yet? Your own dressing-room maybe?'

His voice was cutting and Crystal had an overwhelming urge to throw her mud-caked boots at his beautiful sweater.

'So,' he continued, 'just pretend the room's full of the usual complement of admiring males, watching your strip-tease, which I'm sure you do very fetchingly.'

She sat down heavily on the slatted bench seat.

'You,' she ground out, 'are impossible. This is my work place, and I want you out of it. You've no influence in here.'

'I think you'll find I have, but please ignore me. Change your leggings, and anything else that you care to.'

She stood up and pulled a dry sweater over her head, got her arms stuck, and struggled for what seemed like an age to poke her head out. Her hair broke free and cascaded around her. Furiously, she struggled to restrain it, to restore her dignity.

'Let me help.' The infuriating Farraday man made a move from the doorway.

'Don't you dare!' She backed away. 'I thought you were in a hurry, unless you're going to stay for my bawling out with Bob.'

'I've had my say.'

'So why hang around?' she snapped, shaking out her waterproofs, childishly pleased to see him splattered with raindrops.

'I'm curious to know why a girl like you is working out here in these atrocious conditions. There has to be a good reason, apart from the titillation of being the sole female in a gang of men. Maybe that's the satisfaction you want.'

'If I were a tough, young man, it'd give me great pleasure to knock that insulting remark back down your throat, Mr Farraday, but as I'm only a girl, I couldn't possibly attempt it. In January, site conditions in England are frequently atrocious, as you should know. As for what I'm doing here, you can believe what you like, but I should have thought it was blindingly obvious. However, as it's none of your business anyway, I won't bother to spell it out.'

She stuck her feet into dry boots, bent to ease the laces, and gave him a cool, clear upward freeze of icy eyes.

'I'm sorry about your car. I would have mentioned that earlier if you hadn't been so rude. Now, if you'll excuse me, Mr Farraday, I'll go and see my foreman.'

He stood aside to let her pass but she was close enough to see from the mocking challenge in his blue eyes that he had seen right through her act of bravado. She swept past him, nose high in the air.

Bob Merton put down the phone as she went into his office.

'Crystal, what's all this? It sounds like bad news, I'm afraid. What sort of jam have you got into?'

'Is there any point giving my version?'

Dan Farraday was now standing by the door, and Bob looked from one to the other.

'Sit down, Crystal,' he said. 'Mr Farraday's told me what happened, and I can see the damage done to his car. You staying?'

He looked questioningly at the tall architect.

'Much as I might enjoy the lady's fairy-tale excuses, I'm already late. My insurance company will be in contact with Drummond's. I want to be certain you understand the position. If I come this way again, I do not expect to see this young woman on the site. Understood?'

With one last, comprehensive, sweeping glance at Crystal, he was gone. Neither Crystal nor Bob spoke until they heard the screech of car tyres outside.

'See,' she burst out, 'he drives like a

lunatic. Honestly, Bob, he just shot across in front of me.'

'He says you were driving too fast. Maintains you're not safe on the site, and wants you off the job.'

'That's unfair. He doesn't work here. You're my boss. What's it got to do with him? He has no power . . . '

'I'm afraid he has.' Bob looked uncomfortable. 'You couldn't have picked a worse bloke to run into.'

'Not you, too? Pete told me . . . '

'He's very powerful in our industry. Farraday and Winch are top designers and architects. Winch is practically a sleeping partner now, but he's got influential contacts, and large investments in the UK, and internationally. What makes him so important just now is that Drummond's is tendering for a very big contract to clients of Farraday. So, I've no option. If Dan Farraday wants you sacked, I have to let you go.'

'It's outrageous! Just on his whim? He has no right.'

Crystal stood up, furiously, face-to-face with her foreman.

'Aw, don't be so mad, Crystal. It's just one of those things. Best to go along with him, but I'll see you OK. You're a good worker, too good for what you're doing. You seem to know an awful lot about building, too. You'll easily get another job on site. I'll give you a good reference.'

'That's not the point.' Crystal couldn't help herself. 'I've got to complete this satisfactorily before I can move on. It's important I finish the six months at least. I don't want to . . . '

She stopped, and was aware Bob was eyeing her shrewdly.

'There's something different about you, Crystal Tempest. You're no ordinary on-site worker. What's this all about? I think you'd better come clean.'

She bit her lip. The six months apprenticeship her uncle had demanded was nearly up, all but a week or two. But for that wretched Farraday man it would all have been plain sailing, but now, he'd ruined it all. She knew that if a whiff of this reached her uncle, he'd seize the opportunity to confirm his belief that family in the business always spelled trouble! There was only one route to take. She flicked back her hair, and put on a wheedling expression.

'Bob, I need your help. You're quite right. I couldn't fool you. I'm actually a qualified surveyor. I never actually said I wasn't . . . ' She went on quickly, seeing his expression. 'I desperately needed a job, and — well, you know unc — Mr Drummond's policy. All staff has to start at the bottom, working a stint, no recognition of any qualifications. I had to use much persuasion to get the job, and if this gets back, there'll be no chance of my ever moving on, or making it.'

Bob still eyed her suspiciously, but she was sure he'd no idea she was the mighty Richard Drummond's niece.

'Dan Farraday's out of order going over your head. He's just a blatant chauvinist — obviously despises women!'

'I don't know about that, but he does have a reputation. Hates females in the construction industry — on site, or in the design field.'

'Why?'

'Haven't the faintest, but he can afford whims, his likes and dislikes. His sort usually can. I'll tell you what, Crystal. I'll ring Head Office, and see what they have lined up for you after this. I think I can play this incident down as far as Drummond's is concerned. As for Farraday, just so long as you don't appear here again. Your six months is nearly done, so you'd be moving anyway. He doesn't have to know where.'

'I'd be really grateful.'

Crystal sighed with relief, although she wasn't too sure that Bob was right about the incident going unnoticed. Part of her uncle's success was due to his meticulous attention to detail, but she'd worry about that another day!

'Thanks again, Bob. I'm glad there

are some reasonable men around.'

'Don't judge us all by Dan Farraday. He's probably cooled off by now. Just pretend you work somewhere other than Drummond's if you ever meet him again.'

'Don't worry. As of now, I'm off the Drayton by-pass site, and that's all he asked for, isn't it?'

Crystal didn't tell the rest of the road crew she was leaving. There was no point in complicating the issue, and she couldn't trust herself to speak objectively about Dan Farraday. Every time she thought about him, blazing anger threatened to choke her. She tried to push him out of her mind as she travelled back to town with the other site workers. Jokes were flying about women drivers on site. The crash had made a good story to lighten the winter gloom, but Dan Farraday's image wouldn't go away. The dark thrust of his head, the full mouth, taut with anger, returned again and again throughout the journey back to town.

'Hey! My stop,' she yelled, jolted back to awareness.

They were in Central London, and she always asked to be set down in Hammersmith, and either walked, or took a bus the rest of the way to her flat. To pull up outside her exclusive block of flats would certainly have called for comments from her workmates. Not that it mattered now — she wouldn't be seeing them again.

She slid the van door back, scrambled out into the rainy darkness, and watched the yellow van pull back into the traffic, with mixed feelings. She'd enjoyed her six months. Hard manual labour, and her workouts, had put her in good physical shape, and she was one hundred per cent fitter than on the day she'd asked her uncle for a job.

Trudging along, head down against the driving rain which had started up again with increased ferocity, she promised herself a break that evening — a glass of wine, a long hot bath, a tasty supper with a rich pudding, and, maybe, a chocolate or two afterwards with TV. The thought lent wings to her tired feet.

As she let herself into the carpeted hallway of the flat the telephone was ringing. It was her cousin, Neville Drummond, reminding her of her promise to have supper with him after their regular session at the gym that night. She had clean forgotten about it.

Her encounter with Dan Farraday had really boggled her brain, and it was just as well Neville had phoned. A workout and swim would do more to restore her equilibrium than wine and chocs! Besides, she was fond of her cousin, and knew he was having a hard time at Drummond's.

They met in the foyer of the exclusive Gentleman Jim's Gym, Richard Drummond's very expensive choice for knocking his son and niece into working shape.

'Hi, cousin.' He embraced her fondly, then held her back at arm's length. 'What's up? Something's happened today. You don't look at all like your usual, sunny self. You look all wound up.'

'Does it still show? I'll tell you over supper. Let's get this over and done with. Pain first — pleasure later.'

They both grimaced, but they knew the rules — Richard Drummond's rules!

Crystal sweated her way through a stretch and aerobics class, completed her personal weights programme, and thankfully donned cap and goggles for the final section of her session — thirty lengths in the king-sized pool. This was the fun bit!

With two lengths to go, she slowed, aware of someone coming up very fast behind her. The pool was fairly empty, so there was plenty of room for the swimmer to pass. What she didn't see was another swimmer coming towards them from the opposite direction. Hastily, she moved over to the next lane, but it was too late. The two fast swimmers careered into each other, and both went under water, but not before she'd recognised the one coming towards her. It was Dan Farraday!

She choked at the coincidence. How was it possible for the nightmare of meeting him again to occur within just twelve hours? It just wasn't her day! Nor was it Dan Farraday's, she thought wryly. If he were a nicer man she could almost feel sorry for him, but as it was, all she wanted to do was escape.

She swam quickly to the end of the pool and hauled herself up the steps. With any luck, he would be slanging it out with the other swimmer, arguing the toss as to who was at fault. She left her cap and goggles on, to hide her identity, and hurried towards the changing rooms, clutching a towel round her for greater anonymity.

She was almost at the door when she was spun round. A hand, grasping her towel, unwound her cover. Dan Farraday's eyes registered automatic appreciation, and then something more — a dawning recognition. He made a gesture towards the cap and goggles, putting up a hand as though he would remove them, but Crystal forestalled him. Defiantly, she took them off, her thick hair swinging free.

'You,' he exclaimed, 'again! What are you doing here? This is a members' only club, and you obviously don't know the rules. You were too slow for the fast lane. You're a — a menace, wherever you go. Who brought you here?'

Crystal drew a deep breath. For a few seconds, she couldn't trust herself to speak, and then she looked into the blazing blue of Dan Farraday's anger — for the second time that day! She made a marathon effort to keep her voice calm.

'And I suppose if I tell you whom I came with, you'll exercise your divine right to have me thrown out of here, or else close the club down. It seems no-one's allowed to get in your way, under any circumstance.'

'That's about right.'

She tossed her hair in defiance.

'Go ahead. I'd be interested in the outcome. You've already lost me my job today. Now see what else you can do, Mr Powerful!'

Without realising it, she'd copied his stance, putting her hands on her hips and facing him squarely, locking her eyes with his, in the beginning of a power-struggle which neither intended losing. His unwavering expression caused her eyes to blink. She stepped back, he followed, and for a split second, they almost touched.

'Who,' he repeated, 'brought you here?'

'No-one brought me here. I came here alone, and I've as much right to be here as you. I'm a member, not that it's any of your business, and equally, I could, and probably should, report you for discourtesy and harass-ment.'

His start of surprise gave Crystal satisfaction.

'You were swimming too close. And

you were driving too close to me this afternoon. Are you trying to prove something? Do you always try to crowd women out? Man's in charge — women must submit — that's a philosophy of yours, is it? The woman who dares to argue is sacked. Just like that! Well, I hope today has satisfied your ego. You've put me out of work, but I'll make sure you're not going to spoil my leisure time.'

Dan Farraday didn't look the sort of man who had problems with his ego. His mouth smiled, but his eyes were colder than a Siberian snowscape. He picked up a towel from a lounger and rubbed his dark hair, never taking his eyes off Crystal. Oh, how he reminded her of Dwight Rogers. Bitter memories clouded her eyes. Dan jerked her back to the present, and flung down the towel.

'It gives me no satisfaction at all to see someone lose their job, but you patently weren't safe on that site, and, if you can afford the cost of membership of this place, you don't need to play at slumming on a building site, taking employment from someone really in need. What are you trying to prove? Or are you one of those women who can't bear to be beaten by a man?'

It was fortunate that Neville appeared at that point, or Crystal would certainly have forgotten that she was a lady. Her cousin, fortunately, rescued her from saying something she would surely have recalled later with acute embarrassment.

'Crystal,' Neville said, 'aren't you ready yet? I'm starving. Friend of yours?'

Seemingly unaware of the tension which, to Crystal, seemed thick enough to cut, he smiled at Dan, waiting to be introduced.

'Absolutely not! Just someone who ran into me by mistake — a mistake, I hope, he has no intention of repeating. I shan't be long, Neville. Goodbye, Mr Farraday.'

'Just a minute.'

Dan's sharp command pulled her back.

The two men were eyeing each other curiously. They spoke simultaneously.

'Dan Farraday — the architect?'

'Aren't you Dick Drummond's son?'

Both nodded in answer to the other's question.

Neville, to Crystal's annoyance, put out his hand.

'I'm glad to meet you. Father's spoken very highly of Farraday and Winch.'

'I've known your father professionally for years. He recommended this gym. The one I used to use went bankrupt last month.'

Crystal did a double take. The man's smile was full of friendly warmth, and Neville was positively fawning.

'This one's pretty good. Only the best for Dad.'

Crystal seethed. Another minute and Neville would be asking Dan Farraday to join them for supper, and revealing that she was Dick Drummond's niece.

'I'll see you in the foyer, Neville — five minutes,' she said quickly.

Dan's smile vanished.

'I see now — the connection. So, losing that job's no real problem. I'd say you were amply covered.'

'What's the problem? Crystal's my . . . ' Neville looked puzzled.

His sharp gasp of pain, as Crystal's elbow dug into his ribs, was lost as Crystal spoke.

'Fiancée! Neville and I are engaged, so you see, Mr Farraday, it's quite impossible for you to do me any harm as far as Drummond's is concerned. Isn't that right, Neville? Come along. I'm starving, too.'

She smiled brilliantly up at her cousin, took his arm and marched him out of the pool area. It was as well she couldn't see Dan Farraday's glare at their retreating backs.

At supper, Crystal gave Neville a watered-down version of her day, swearing him to secrecy where his father was concerned.

'Fat chance I get to talk to him at all these days. He blames me for losing that local authority contract. But why do I have fiancé status all of a sudden? What's with you and this guy, Farraday?'

'Nothing. I don't know why I said that, except that I didn't want him to know I was part of the family. Forget it, Neville.'

'If you say so. Just let me know when we're through, and I'm free again. This could seriously cramp my style.'

Crystal giggled.

'I'm sorry, Neville. Sure I'll release you — any time. It's that man. He just got under my skin. I can't stand his type.'

'He's an amazing architect apparently, and very powerful in his field.'

'If anybody else tells me that again, I'll scream. Now, don't mention him again. I want to enjoy what's left of the day. Let's talk about you, and our campaign to get you out of Drummond's and into Art College. Much more your line.'

'Dad'll never allow me out. I'm having to pay for making the mistake of thinking I wanted to be a surveyor in the first place.'

'Oh, I don't know. He can be quite persuadable.'

'Maybe, for you, but not for me. Drummond's a life sentence for me. Crazy really, because when Dad does condescend to talk to me, he's always telling me what a liability I am to the organisation. Maybe he's punishing me. He just hates family in the business. I don't know how you got away with it.'

'Unlike you, I just love the job,' Crystal replied, thinking that Dan Farraday wouldn't put up with anything he disliked for more than ten seconds, but then, his sort of man was a cold, ruthless egotist as well. She just hoped their paths would never cross again.

Richard Drummond's phone call next morning helped to erase the previous day's disaster from her mind. She'd slept late for the first time in months, and struggled to clear her head.

'Uncle Dick? How nice of you to call.'

She was tentative. How much had he been told? Was it the end of her hopes at Drummond's?

'It's not a social call.'

He sounded testy, and her heart sank.

'Strictly work. I told you — none of the family stuff.'

'No, sir — er — Mr Drummond.'

'No sarcasm either. I've got a very positive report here from Bob Merton. He's pleased with you. Buckled down well, and no disasters so far!'

She held her breath.

'Job finished a day or so early, so he's letting you go, but you've done OK. So, you can shift to the bottom rung of the managerial ladder — Assistant Site Manager for a new project. In the early stages as yet, so you can be in at the beginning. Come into the office this morning, pick up the details, and

50

Crystal . . . I'm still not your uncle, officially.

'Unofficially, I hope you'll be at my birthday party at the end of next month. I'm giving you lots of notice because your folks'll be there, too. Now, good luck with Brinscombe Manor Park. Do well there and, who knows, I might have my niece back soon, once you've proved yourself to be a Drummond, if that's what you want.'

He rang off, and Crystal let out a yell of happy triumph.

'Bless you, Uncle Dick and Bob Merton, and blow you, Dan Farraday!'

3

Crystal was even more delighted next morning when she presented herself for briefing at Drummond's Site Management Headquarters and picked up details of her new job. Brinscombe Manor Park was an innovative and ambitious project backed by a prestigious financial consortium which had acquired a sizeable chunk of land in Berkshire.

Manor Park was a housing experiment based on the old English village concept, with a mix and match of houses for professionals, young marrieds and retired folk — a community cross section. At the centre of the development there was a large leisure complex, with outdoor and indoor swimming pools.

The outline drawings reminded Crystal of developments she'd worked on in the States. Sun City in Arizona came into her mind, though that had been designed for retired people, and although she'd been fascinated by the concept, the memory wasn't pleasant.

Dwight had taken her there on business, then they'd had a week in Las Vegas. It was in Vegas that Crystal had imagined she'd fallen in love with him, and gone on to doubt her own judgment ever since. Would she ever be able to forget that ghastly year? She shook her head to clear it of the past, and concentrated on the job in hand.

As Assistant Site Manager at Brinscombe Manor, she'd be in charge of labour and supplies, a sort of general administrative dogsbody, with maybe the possibility of influencing design. After the Drayton bypass, it'd be a piece of cake. She couldn't believe her luck — until she saw the name of the architects on the preliminary plans! Farraday and Winch!

As soon as she saw the name, she visualised Dan Farraday storming out of his red Porsche, and then looming over her at the poolside. But the site manager, Jim Reynolds, reassured her.

'Farraday? Unlikely you'll bump into him. He runs the whole firm now, and he's abroad a lot, wheeling and dealing, rather than actually designing. Brinscombe Manor's just fairly straightforward construction now, though I believe he negotiated with Mr Drummond himself when he tendered for the job. Only just got it, too. Dan Farraday and the old man get on like a house on fire. Mr Drummond was helpful in Farraday's early days, before he bought into Winch.'

Crystal breathed a sigh of relief and vowed not to look again at the name stamped on every plan of the Brinscombe Manor complex!

As the days went by, she felt easier about the possibility of running into Dan Farraday. It seemed only slight, and even when Jim called her into the office and told her to stand in for him at a planning conference with the architects next day, Dan Farraday was not in her thoughts.

She'd spoken on the phone to Vincent Wain, the architect in charge of the project. The meeting was scheduled for nine o'clock at the offices of Farraday and Winch, and she assumed Dan was out of the country. In any case, the red Porsche incident was over two months ago, and surely even Dan Farraday couldn't keep a grudge going for ever.

Crystal was pleased with herself. The meeting went smoothly. She'd introduced her site team to the consortium clients, and Vincent Wain, a young, fresh-faced young architect, had struck up a good rapport with her. He was bringing the meeting to a close.

'That wraps it up for now,' he said. 'Work begins in eight weeks.'

Timing had been the only slight problem. The consortium had wanted an immediate start. Crystal, for reasons she couldn't fathom, had been instructed to delay as long as possible, without arousing suspicion that there were any problems.

'What problems?' she'd asked, but Jim Reynolds had evaded her question, and she'd won the point for Drummond's, without a late-start penalty clause, too. For herself, she was so excited by the project she'd have liked to start that very day!

A door behind her opened, and she was aware of a subtle change of atmosphere in the room which raised the hairs on her neck. She knew who it was before the familiar silky dark voice spoke.

'Not quite all, Vincent. I'm not too happy about the last thing I head. Eight weeks delay — not in our client's best interests, at all. Several of those houses have already been sold, off the drawing-board, and the sooner we're up and running, the sooner the cash flows in for the clients. You should know that. I'd like to know Drummond's reasons for this delay.'

'Mr Farraday! I thought you were in Portugal.'

'All tied up there. Thought I'd see how Brinscombe Park was coming along. Seems a magic-tongued operator has persuaded you to buy more time for Drummond's. I'm intrigued.'

Crystal didn't turn around. With her hair piled high, and wearing a smart red jacket, she knew she was unrecognisable, from behind, as the figure in oilskins on the Drayton roadworks. But, of course, Dan Farraday came into the room to shake hands with his clients from the consortium, turned round, and looked straight into her eyes.

The flare of recognition was intense. Her own eyes widened, anticipating a tiger pounce, but he merely put his hands in his pockets and nodded towards his clients.

'Well, gentlemen, if you're satisfied, we won't detain you. I'll thrash out the last point myself, and we'll be in touch. Perhaps I may be present at the next meeting, on site, I hope, very soon.'

Smiling, he ushered them out of the office, his backward glance telling Crystal and Vincent to stay exactly where they are. When he came back the smile had vanished.

'Now, Vincent, perhaps you'll explain what Miss Tempest is doing here.'

'She works for Drummond's, of course. She's . . . '

'I know what she is, or was. Has Sir Richard gone totally mad? Since when did the labourers meet our clients? What is going on here? It's not too late to withdraw the contract from Drummond's. The whole thing is preposterous.'

He punched the intercom.

'Liz, get me Richard Drummond, in person — right now!'

'Hold on,' Vincent interrupted. 'I'm sorry, Mr Farraday, but there's obviously a mistake of some sort.'

'There surely is, and I'm about to rub it out. Drummond's are about to pay.'

'But Crystal isn't a labourer!'

Crystal cut in swiftly, 'Thanks, Vincent, but I can speak for myself. Mr Farraday, I'm Assistant Site Manager for the Brinscombe Manor project. You'll find my qualifications and experience more than adequate for the job. If you want a copy of my c.v., Drummond's will supply it.'

The silence was the sort which frequently preceded a thunderstorm. Crystal thought that every time she encountered Dan Farraday, the barometer was set stormy! Slowly, he took his finger from the switch.

'Liz, cancel that call, for the moment.'

To Vincent, he said, 'I'll see you later. You,' he said, staring directly at Crystal, 'I'd like to see in my office right now.'

She flushed, resenting his manner, feeling like a naughty schoolgirl.

'I do have other work to do,' she protested, with as much dignity as she could muster.

'Forget it,' he said simply, striding out of the room. 'Just follow me.'

She hesitated, looking ruefully at Vincent.

'Best do as he says. We all do, and,' he added with a smile, 'it usually turns out for the best. Blast him!'

Crystal stepped out after the retreating back but, by the time she had reached the office, he was coming back down the corridor, shrugging on a leather jacket.

'What . . . ?' she began.

'Come on, we'll talk outside. I've been cooped up in a plane for the last few hours. I need some air. And you are going to explain yourself. Come on.'

Farraday and Winch's offices were centrally placed in the City of London. Dan Farraday strode across the busy street outside, but Crystal deliberately kept a few paces behind, half inclined to turn around and return to her own office at Drummond's.

He turned up a quiet side street and, a few hundred yards along, ducked down some steps, pushed open a door and held it for her, an impatient frown on his face.

'Come on, I haven't got all day.'

Her hair grazed his sleeve as she was about to pass under his arm. She stopped and looked coldly up at him.

'This is my lunch hour, Mr Farraday, and a meeting with you isn't on my schedule today. You practically forced me to accompany you. I've seen Vincent, and your clients. They are happy enough. I've nothing more to say to you at present.'

'I'm going to find out what you're up to, and I'm hungry. So, if you'll go in, I'll buy us lunch,' he snapped.

'Not for me, thanks, and I'm not up to anything. That's a ridiculous assumption.'

He replied more evenly, softly.

'So, if you're not up to anything, you'll have no objection to prolonging your business with the firm through lunch.'

'I suppose not,' she muttered, thrown by his change of tone.

The wine bar was crowded, but Dan easily commandeered a discreetly placed booth, where they could see, but not be seen. He was the sort of man who always would find the perfect spot, catch the waiter's immediate attention, she thought resentfully.

'I'll get my own drink,' she said.

'Sit down, please. You don't have to prove anything. What will you have?'

'Mineral water then, please.'

'To eat?'

She shook her head, but he returned with a piled plate of smoked salmon sandwiches, a whisky and her mineral water. She sipped her mineral water, and watched as he bit into a sandwich. The silence was unnerving. Finally, she could stand it no longer.

'Well?' she said abruptly. 'You've dragged me in here. What do you want?'

'Hardly dragged you.'

The pile of sandwiches was fast disappearing. He pushed the plate towards her, but she shook her head.

He leaned back, arms folded, tilting back his chair away from her, frowning, eyes narrowed.

'You're trouble, Crystal Tempest, and you're beginning to get in my hair. Every time I bump into you, it's a disaster area. That collision at Drayton, I could just about accept as a stupid error of judgment on your part. The accident at the gym could have been coincidence, maybe, but when you turn up on my own doorstep, purporting to be site manager on one of my projects — in spite of the fact that you're supposed to be off Drummond's pay roll — even you must admit, it begins to look a trifle odd.'

Crystal continued to stare coldly at him, but apprehension was spreading through to the pit of her stomach. This man was a power within the industry, and he could be a terrible obstacle in her struggle to re-establish her professional life. She disliked him, but couldn't afford to antagonise him further, both for her own sake and her uncle's.

The bitter lesson she'd learned in America still dogged her. There, it had been rash impulsiveness which had ruined her personal life and career prospects. She had to rebuild that life. Dan Farraday was a menace who needed careful handling. Surely she'd learned some wisdom in the last year, some communication skills.

'Answers,' he repeated. 'Specifically, number one, why were you masquerading as a site labourer at Drayton? Number two, how do you explain your rapid promotion to site manager, and on the rather special Brinscombe Manor project, too? Lastly, for the moment, what on earth are Drummond's playing at, delaying the start time on this contract? Vincent has some explaining to do also.'

'It wasn't Vincent's fault,' she rushed hotly. 'Your clients were agreeable.'

'I suppose you used your sex appeal, which I have to admit is considerable, to persuade them it was in their best interests to go along with you. Just how far are you prepared to push your femininity to get what you want? Is that why you're in this business? Does it give you an ego trip to be a woman in what is virtually a man's field, where there's no competition?'

Crystal stood up, fury sparking from her dark eyes.

'I don't need to take this, Mr Farraday. You are insulting and chauvinistic. What's your problem, I wonder. Why is it so hard for you to deal with a woman? Can't you see beyond the female form?'

Curious glances were turned towards their table. Crystal's voice was stormy, and she leaned forward. Standing, she was about eye level with Dan, near enough to see the few fine silver wires in his dark curls, near enough to see the dark irises in his eyes, which were blazing with furious anger and contempt.

It was the contempt which startled

her, and then she saw something else which completely threw her — anguished, naked pain, the sort that had so often startled her in her own mirrored reflection during the past months. It sobered her and brought a strange sympathetic empathy to know Dan Farraday had, or was even now suffering, just as she had.

She lowered her eyes. She didn't want to see that. He took advantage of her hesitation, reached across and gripped her wrists, pressing down, pushing her back into her seat.

'Sit down, Crystal! We're not through yet.'

She pulled away, but it was only when he chose to release her that she could move. Pain circled her wrists, but she endured it, rather than give him the satisfaction of seeing her trying to ease it with massage. She put her hands under the table, flexed her fingers, and sat perfectly still, willing the fire to die away.

'What more do you need to know?'

she said after a silence which seemed to last for ages. 'I work for Drummond's, not for you, so, please, I must go.'

He pounced, as she knew he would.

'Drummond's works for me, and my clients, on this project. I can cancel the contract at any time. You'd know that, if you've read the small print.'

'No, I haven't. The legal, contractual obligations are nothing to do with me. My job is Assistant Site Manager, construction and design. Surely you know the workings of the industry, Mr Farraday!'

'Don't get smart. You should know every detail of every contract, and don't you forget, design of the Brinscombe Manor complex is absolutely nothing to do with Drummond's. You don't interfere at all. Your job is construction to our design.'

Crystal thought hard, and took a deep breath. It was hopeless. He was challenging her on every front. Something was eating him, deep down, apart from all the things he thought she was guilty of. But she had to be careful. He could wipe out all the careful pre-planning and work Drummond's had already put in, at the snap of his fingers!

The Brinscombe Manor contract had been won by a whisker, based on her uncle's formidable personality and, it seemed, his personal link with Dan Farraday. She couldn't jeopardise it. For the firm's sake, she had to bury her animosity, or at least conceal it. Lifting her head, she squared her shoulders, hair rippling back from her face, and looked directly into the eyes of the enemy.

'Perhaps I should explain, Mr Farraday. It seems we've got off on the wrong foot. I didn't intend it and I'm sorry for any inconvenience it's caused.'

She was all sweet reasonableness, but her wrists still stung and she was fighting mad. Dan Farraday watched her, his dark eyes suspicious.

'The Drayton by-pass job,' she went on. 'That's easy. You must have heard of Sir Richard's methods. All management jobs are earned after a start at the bottom. If you can't do what you ask the others to do, you're not worth hiring. I agree with that.'

'So, you can do anything any of the men can do — scaffolding, roofing, pipe laying, drive the cranes, the JCBs?'

He was being provocatively sceptical.

'I can do any of that, yes, but they're specialists' jobs. I would only step in where necessary.'

'All right then. Why were you at the swimming pool that same evening?'

'What does that have to do with my work? That was pure coincidence.'

'You weren't deliberately tailing me?'

'Goodness, no! Why should I do that?'

'That's what I intend to find out. To get your job back, perhaps?'

'What!'

It was a relief, after all the tension, to laugh. But Dan was not amused. His dark brows clouded. He leaned forward, and for a second, Crystal thought he was going to touch her. She drew back.

'It's true what I told you at your office,' she said quickly. 'I'm well qualified. You can have my c.v.'

'I'm not interested. I'm sure Dick Drummond isn't such a fool as to employ novices.'

He stopped and a hard light diffused the dark pupils. He leaned back, then smashed his fist into his palm with such force, Crystal jumped.

'Of course! What a fool! I'd forgotten. Well, well. I've always admired Drummond — a man of complete integrity, a rare thing nowadays in business. Or so I thought. What a disappointment! No wonder you're on a cushy, upmarket, desirable work number like Brinscombe Manor. You're engaged to Neville Drummond — the boss's son. That puts an entirely different complexion on things.'

He stood up, contempt on his face, his eyes raking her from head to toe.

'You're quite a looker, Crystal Tempest,' he said slowly, 'and you certainly know how to use it to advantage.'

She'd stood up, and now came round the table to face him, swinging her arm back to strike. He'd made her so mad she forgot all caution, but with a laugh, he caught her arm in mid air, and slowly forced it down, pulling her against him as he did so. They were well concealed by the high, wooden booths, but Crystal saw that he wouldn't have cared if the entire room had been watching them. His iron grip didn't slacken, as he pinioned her other arm across his waist.

'No, Crystal — that's not such a good idea.'

He spoke very softly, but every syllable counted, and fear returned. Would she never learn to curb her impulsiveness? For seconds she was clamped to him, then he released her, and smiled.

'Well,' he said mildly, 'I do believe you were about to use physical violence against me. Don't overdo the macho, Crystal. It doesn't become you, and it doesn't intimidate me at all.'

He was laughing at her! Crystal picked up her bag, whirled around to face him, fighting for control.

'Go to blazes, Mr Farraday. I hope we never meet again.'

'That will be difficult, as you'll be working for me for at least the next twelve months. See you at Brinscombe Manor, Miss Tempest — in a better temper, I hope!'

She hurried out of the wine bar, and into the street, hearing his laughter behind her, smarting with the knowledge that Dan Farraday had won that particular round.

4

The last hour had been a nightmare. Crystal glanced back, half expecting to see the tall figure chasing her, but there was no sign of him. A cup of coffee in a nearby café gave her respite, black coffee and a slice of pizza. Strange how hungry she'd suddenly become.

As the caffeine restored her nerve, Crystal wondered what to do next. She'd been very rude to a man of importance to Drummond's. Regrettable, but it had been impossible to bow down to Dan Farraday. He'd been looking for a confrontation, and it seemed to happen every time they met. He had the upper hand, and he knew it — he could destroy her!

It was probable that, even now, he was on the telephone to Uncle Dick demanding that Crystal Tempest be sacked — again! She couldn't help a wry smile now she'd calmed down. Maybe she was fated not to work for Drummond's. Uncle Dick could well be proved right, and that family in business was trouble. But Crystal knew she was good at her job. It was her rash behaviour which kept getting her into trouble, and her inability to keep quiet if she felt unjustly treated.

She sighed. She never used to be like that. It was only since the American fiasco she'd been so wary and jumpy. She didn't trust anyone since Dwight Roger's betrayal, but neither did she trust herself. Perhaps she never would again. She'd forgotten all about being engaged to Neville, too! They'd jokingly called it off a week after their meeting at the gym, when they met for a drink.

'I can't be lumbered with you as my fiancée, Crystal dear, much as I love you. You see, I've met this girl, Carla.'

'I release you, and I'd like to meet Carla. How serious is this one?'

'Pretty serious. Oh, I know I've said that before, but Carla's special.'

'Uncle Dick? Has he met her?'

'You're joking. We're still not really on speaking terms. I shall never be free of Drummond's, you know. He's punishing me by making me stay there now. I hardly dare put pen to drawing-board lest I make another mistake.'

'It wasn't so dreadful. Lots of us have got the costings wrong on a job.'

'Unfortunately mine was sent out to the client, the County Council. Good job for me it wasn't a private body which could have held us to the costings. As it happened, it just made Drummond's, and me in particular, the Managing Director's son, look incompetent idiots! Dad would've sacked anyone else on the spot, but I have to stay and be humiliated. Teach me a lesson!'

'Don't give up. It was a long time ago now, and you haven't put a foot wrong since. We'll think of something.'

She came back to the present with a jolt. Neville's problems and solving them wasn't going to help her own situation, and it was no good moping. Best to get back to the office and see whether Mr Big had put in his powerful oar, yet again!

'How did it go, from your angle?' Jim Reynolds greeted her when she finally got back to the office.

'Er, OK. Vincent's a pet, and the clients seem happy, but . . . '

'But what?'

'Dan Farraday turned up. You said he wouldn't be involved in the Brinscombe Manor project.'

'I shouldn't have thought so, but he's a law unto himself, and since Winch gave up he does have a growing reputation for keeping a finger in all the firm's pies.'

'I wish I'd known. We don't seem to get on, on a personal level. Best if I keep right out of the way. Women, this woman anyway, seem to get under his skin.'

'So I've heard. He has an aversion to them on the actual sites.'

'I wonder he can get away with it in this day and age.'

'I've also heard he's a bit of a law to himself. He did phone, actually.'

'Oh, no! Now what?'

'That much of an ogre, was he? Actually, he hardly mentioned you. It was the delayed start date he was angry about. You were only carrying out orders from high on that one. I told him that, and he accepted it.'

'Really? He could have fooled me.' She could hardly believe it. 'You mean he doesn't want me off the job?'

'Why should he? I got the impression he has far bigger things to worry about. No disrespect to you, Crystal.'

'None taken.'

She stretched her arms in elation. Saved again!

'He did say something odd though. Not at all in character. Something about the bad penny of Brinscombe Manor probably going to make him bankrupt. Was it some kind of joke I missed?'

'No, it's no joke. He means it.'

Crystal's elation vanished.

Next morning was chaotic in her small section of Drummond Construction. The boss himself, Sir Richard, had ordered the work on Brinscombe Manor to start immediately.

'And that means today,' Jim said to his team which he'd assembled first thing that morning. 'We have to be on site today. Drop everything else you're working on. Give this priority.'

'But why?' someone asked.

'I thought you wanted a delay?' came another voice.

'I'd shelved it.'

Jim ignored all other comments and questions.

'I've been instructed by Sir Richard and Dan Farraday. So, let's get moving.'

And move they did. Crystal was on site later in the morning, and had the special cabins set up, for administrations and stores, all installed completely by evening. She spent most of the day on the phone, rounding up contractors and materials. All day, and during the next few days, she expected Dan Farraday to turn up to complain or fault-find, or worse still, order her off the site publicly! But the days passed, and it was Vincent she dealt with.

They got on well together. He asked her to have dinner with him a couple of times, but she found an excuse. She liked him well enough, but as a working partner. The last thing she needed in her life was emotional and professional entanglement.

Crystal didn't dare tempt fate by mentioning Dan Farraday's name, but it was Vincent who put her mind at rest, when he casually mentioned that the boss had suddenly taken off for an island in the Pacific. She sighed with relief. She could stop looking over her shoulder for a while at least.

'Holiday or work?' she asked nonchalantly.

'Both, I think. Spur-of-the-moment thing. Some multi-millionaire friend has hatched up a scheme, and apparently sent his personal jet to pick up Mr Farraday and friends. Lucky them!'

'Oh, come on, Brinscombe Manor's not so bad. Tell you what, I'll share my sandwiches with you to celebrate the first footings going in.'

'I was hoping for a more exotic celebration than a sandwich — tonight perhaps, after work?'

'Oh, Vincent, I'm sorry. I . . . er . . . have a date tonight.'

She started to babble about bathroom fittings, and wished she had the courage to tell him her date was with Gentleman Jim, and furthermore, she had absolutely no interest in romance of any sort at present.

'I shall keep asking,' was all he said, but his crestfallen expression made Crystal feel sad and guilty in one go.

She found, to her annoyance, that her thoughts were more on the infuriating Dan Farraday. As well as a feeling of relief that he wouldn't be popping up, she had almost a twinge of envy. Who were those friends, she wondered.

The following day, Sir Richard Drummond made a surprise visit to the site. Jim Reynolds was away, Crystal was in charge, and had been frantically busy all day. Work was progressing so well she'd realised she was in danger of running short of concrete. At short notice, it was hard to make sure the huge mixers arrived on time, and at the right time. Sir Richard came into the office to hear the end of her persuasive spiel on the telephone.

'Jacob, if you could get it here tomorrow, I'll give you the biggest hug when we meet. Sure — soon I expect. You're a genius — a miracle! 'Bye now.' She hung up and, turning, recognised her visitor.

'Unc . . . Sir Richard . . . !'

'Ugh!' His derisive snort made her smile. 'Using your feminine wiles, eh? You little minx!'

'They do work sometimes. Good for something, we are.'

'Never said you weren't. It's family in

81

the firm I object to, not women in general.'

There was no-one else in the office, but Crystal, warningly, put her fingers to her lips. It was rare to have a quiet second. Dick waved his hand.

'Oh, you can forget all the secrecy. Truth to tell, I'm pleased with you. I might not have been in daily touch, but I've monitored every minute of your working days.' He cleared his throat, and said gruffly, 'I admit, I was wrong — maybe,' he hedged, 'in your case. Quite an asset to the organisation, unlike my son. I'm proud of you, girl. You're working wonders here.'

Crystal felt a lump in her throat, and would have dearly loved to rush over and hug him. But this was working time — he wouldn't approve. But at least her professional life was going well!

'Thanks, Uncle,' she said quietly. 'I'm pleased you're pleased. I'd still like to keep our connection quiet though, not to make a thing of it.'

'Up to you. No need to announce it,

but I thought I'd tell you that the probationary period's over, and I'm happy to acknowledge my niece again.'

'Great! I'm sorry, by the way, about the start date. I don't understand why, but I'd worked on the clients and on Vincent, from Farraday's. They were agreeable, then the big boss came in, and was furious.'

She looked enquiringly at him, and it was then she noticed that he didn't look his usual robust self.

'Uncle Dick, you don't look so well. Is anything wrong?'

Dick Drummond had always enjoyed perfect health, and Crystal couldn't remember him ever being ill. She looked closer, noticing he was more drawn.

'Nothing wrong. Don't fuss.' He sounded testy. 'I'm not getting any younger.'

'Not you, Uncle, you're in your prime. Have you been overworking?'

'Yes, yes, maybe a bit. Don't fuss,' he repeated. 'The new start date's fine, as it happens. Farraday also put in a late finish penalty payment clause. I out-manoeuvred him there though. If we finish early, which he reckons impossible, he has to pay us. How's that for a deal? And with you on it, the way it's going, it's looking good. Keep it up, girl. Now, let's have a look round.'

Crystal put on her hard hat, and turned as they left the office cabin.

'I'd still rather it not be known that you're my uncle,' she said.

'Right. Lead on, lady. Oh, by the way, don't forget my birthday party, will you? Your folks'll be here Friday. Can't wait to see them Saturday. And I hear Neville's got a new girl. He's promised to bring her to the party. I wouldn't admit it to anyone but you, and don't dare tell him this, but he's keeping his nose to the grindstone pretty well lately. Maybe I've been a bit hard on him.'

'He's anxious to please you, I do know that,' Crystal replied, thinking it was ridiculous for the two of them not to get on together.

She was relieved to see that Dick looked more like his old self now, smiling and confident, ready to take on the world. Her fears vanished. It had just been a bad moment. Things were looking good. If only Dan Farraday would stay on his Pacific island for ever . . .

When Dan did eventually return, his first work call was at Brinscombe Park. Crystal was off site all that day, visiting building suppliers with a long list of problems and queries she and Jim had put together. She didn't get back to site until well past the working end of the day, but Jim was still there.

'Crystal! I thought you'd never get here. Farraday's been!'

'No! That'll put the finishing touches to a perfect day.'

'Problems?'

'Quite a few, but tell me yours first. I expect yours are greater than mine — if he's been visiting.'

'Not so, just the reverse. Dan Farraday is one hundred per cent satisfied with the progress. He brought along a couple of consortium top brass, too, and they were beside themselves with delight. Mind you, they should be pleased. We're a couple of weeks ahead of schedule already.'

'Well, I'm glad I missed the visit. If I'd been here, Farraday would certainly have found something to beef about!'

'No, credit where it's due. I told him things are so spot on, because you are so meticulous about working exactly to the Farraday and Winch specifications.'

'Have to admit, they are pretty good. What did he say to that?'

'I couldn't make it out. Kinda growled.'

'Bet he did. Well, I'm glad he was pleased. A major breakthrough for me! Let's forget him now. I've brought a whole new set of problems back . . . '

Oblivious of the fact that Jim Reynolds had a wife and family to get home to, she was off, launching into what she loved doing best — marrying first-class construction with super-class design. Her respect and admiration for Farraday and Winch was as great as her dislike of Farraday the man. Because of the quality of the man's work, her own job was totally absorbing, so much so, she could actually forget, for a while, that there was still unfinished business back in the States . . .

5

Crystal flicked through the post. It used to be one of life's pleasures. Anything could lie in the assortment of envelopes on the mat. Even though it was usually mainly junk mail or bills, the anticipation didn't lessen.

Nowadays, she dreaded the post, especially anything from America. Dwight Rogers had killed even that simple pleasure. There was one airmail letter but it was from Spain, in her mother's familiar handwriting, probably giving the flight arrival time at Heathrow. Nothing from the States. Another day's reprieve!

She slit open her mother's letter. Crystal was looking forward to seeing her parents. It was nearly a year since she'd visited them in Spain, just after her return from Nevada. Then her main concern had been to conceal her unhappiness. She'd even cut short her visit when her mother had started asking probing questions. It was hard to fool Helen Tempest, and Crystal's wounds had been too raw to expose even to her loving mother.

Now, since working at Drummond's, her confidence and self-esteem partially restored, she looked forward to sharing her anxieties with her parents. She knew she could count on her mother's calm and sympathetic support and her father would be full of reassuring practical advice. She couldn't wait to see them! Uncle Dick had invited her to stay at his mansion overlooking Hampstead Heath for his birthday party weekend.

There was plenty of room for her parents to stay in the gorgeous flat she was enjoying, but it was on the fourth floor with no wheelchair access, now essential for her father. After the accident at Drummond's which had left Jack Tempest a paraplegic, Dick Drummond had had an apartment specially converted on the ground floor of his house with every facility to make life easier for his injured brother-in-law.

Helen and Jack had stayed a while, but when Dick bought a villa in Spain, similarly converted, they'd found the climate and lifestyle suited them so well their London visits became more and more rare.

Crystal just had time to skim her mother's letter before she left for work, though she was cutting it a bit fine. She had an early appointment with the landscape contractor. But there was disappointment as she read the news. Her parents weren't going to make it for the party. Her father wasn't fit enough.

A minor setback, her mother wrote, *but you know your dad. Unless he's feeling one hundred per cent he's scared to death of being a nuisance. 'Course, he's pushing me to go alone, but I don't want to do that. We'll fly over as soon as he's well again and we'll have our own private birthday party with Dick. I'll ring him on the day, and I'll expect a letter from you with every detail. Dick's parties are a shame to miss.*

Crystal stuffed the letter in her bag. She hoped it was only a minor setback. Her mother was an expert at making light of things. As soon as she had a couple of days off, Crystal vowed to go and see for herself, though the pace at the Brinscombe Manor site was too frantic to allow time off at the moment.

Bad start, bad day! The landscape contractor was late, and proved a difficult character with his own ideas on where to plant the screening copses of trees and bushes. Unfortunately, they differered from the Farraday and Winch specifications. Crystal wondered why Vincent had chosen this particular awkward fellow!

'It'd be better to site these on the west side of the sports complex,' he announced.

'No! Mr Farraday's instructions are explicit. In the position you suggest, 'don't you see, evening light would be cut down on the west-facing terraces.'

She pointed out on the plans the swirling patterns of greenery, cunningly placed to convince Brinscombe Manor's fortunate residents they were living in almost rural surroundings. The contractor looked doubtful.

'Mr Farraday won't mind. Most architects are glad to defer to their landscapers. Bricks and mortar's their job — planting's mine. I'll give him a ring.'

'No. Mr Farraday isn't like most architects and he's not the type to defer to anyone. I'll mention your idea to Vincent Wain, but for now I'd prefer you to work to the specifications.'

She finally got rid of him, still grumbling, and with relief turned to the practical details of her job. She climbed a ladder to check on some suspect roofing timber. Vincent yelled from ground level.

'Crystal, can you come down a sec?'

Vincent hadn't been due a site visit.

What was up now?

'I'll just finish here. Won't be long.'

She tapped the wooden beam, ran her fingers over the rough surface and squinted along its length. Scrambling along the framework, she examined it from end to end, and thought for a few minutes. The carpenter watched her anxiously.

'Ben, this isn't the graded timber I ordered. It's rubbish. How did it get in here?'

'Dunno. It's part of the last delivery from the timber merchants.'

'Well, I'm sorry, but it won't do. Did you check the load?'

'Yep. Must have missed that though.'

'Strip it out. It's not worth the risk.'

'It'll take time.'

'We're way ahead of schedule. Better deal with it now rather than later. See what you can do.'

She gave him a dazzling smile.

'OK, Crystal, seeing it's you.'

Ramming her hard hat more firmly

round her ears, she climbed back down the ladder.

'Vincent! Trouble? I didn't expect you today,' she greeted him.

'No trouble. I'm on a job near Reading. Brinscombe was on my route so I thought I'd pop in and ask you something.'

'You seem mighty cheerful about whatever it is.'

'I am.'

He waved an embossed card.

'An invitation from Sir Dick Drummond himself — to his birthday party. I met him with Dan at preliminary meetings about Brinscombe Manor, but never thought he'd invite me to his party. It's for Vincent Wain and friend. Will you come with me?'

'Er . . . well . . . actually, I am already going.'

'You! I didn't know you knew the great man. I suppose you're already going with someone.'

'I was going with my parents, but they can't make it.'

'No boyfriend?' Vincent's eyes shone with hope.

'No, and not interested. You know the score on that. I told you before.'

'So no harm in going with me then, just as a friend? No harm, no strings?'

'Oh, OK, if you're going anyway. Just as long as you understand it's purely as a friend. Oh, I'm meeting a couple of people for a drink before the party. D'you want to come along?'

Safety in numbers, she thought.

★ ★ ★

Neville had asked her to have a drink before the party so he could introduce her to Carla.

'For moral support,' he explained. 'She's terrified of meeting Dick the Dragon! As far as I can see, the whole of London's been invited. I can't think what Dad's playing at. He doesn't usually go in for these crush affairs.'

'It's his birthday, so it's up to him.

Oh, and, Neville, try to avoid the cousin label, will you?'

'Still travelling incognito, are you?'

'I prefer it, though Uncle Dick doesn't seem to mind now.'

'I'll try to remember not to be too familiar.'

As it turned out, there was little danger. All Neville's attention was for Carla, a very pretty green-eyed blonde, a nurse, whose warm, friendly personality sparked the evening off to a good start. When Vincent and Neville ordered drinks at the bar, she confided her worries about Dick Drummond to Crystal.

'He sounds such an ogre. Poor Neville's life is quite shadowed by him.'

'They're going through a bad patch just now, but Uncle Dick's a sweetie when you get to know him.'

Carla looked at Crystal curiously.

'Neville's told me about you being a Drummond. I shan't let on of course. Don't you work with Vincent?'

'Yes. It's a bit silly trying to keep it a

secret. After all, I've served my apprenticeship.'

'You've done wonders, according to Neville.'

'Oh, he's a bit biased. He doesn't like working at Drummond's, but my work's a pleasure. I love it!'

'Lucky you.' Carla grimaced. 'I'm on early shift tomorrow, so I won't be able to stay at the party long.'

'That's a shame. You mustn't miss the buffet. It's usually spectacular!'

'Let's hurry those men up with the drinks then and let's get going.'

Carla laughed, and Crystal could understand why her cousin seemed to be falling head over heels in love.

Sir Richard Drummond's large circular drive was littered with impressive, expensive cars, and the house lights blazed golden over Hampstead Heath.

'Wowee,' Carla said as she clutched Neville's arm, 'this is a seriously rich place. I'm scared.'

'Probably all this stuff's in hock to the bank, and I'm poor as a mouse.

Let's get the introduction over with. See you later, Crystal, when the scrum's thinned.'

Crystal knew her uncle always turned this sort of affair over to first-class caterers. His birthday party was always a lavish affair, but never before on this scale. Dick usually preferred a more manageable number. It was incredibly noisy, and once they were in the main reception hall with its glittering chandeliers, it was very hot. Waiters manoeuvred skilfully amongst the throng balancing trays of champagne.

Vincent took a couple of glasses and offered one to Crystal.

'I'd prefer a fruit juice at the moment. I'm very thirsty.'

'OK, I'll go find you one. Hold on to this.'

Crystal found a convenient pillar to stand by while she waited for him. She saw her uncle by the drawing-room, leaning attentively to listen to Carla. He looked pleased, and even managed to include Neville in his smile.

They all chatted for a few minutes, then the young pair were swept away by a group of serious-faced men in dinner jackets — business colleagues, Crystal guessed. She waved, caught her uncle's eye, mouthed, 'Happy birthday, see you later,' and blew him a kiss. He shrugged, grimaced, took out a large handkerchief and mopped his brow. He looked hot and worried.

Vincent came back with a glass of chilled mango juice.

'Sorry I was so long. Devil of a job to move about. There's a fabulous spread in a sort of state room! Oh, Neville says to tell you he'll be taking Carla home shortly, then he'll be back.'

'Maybe we should eat then, before it's too late.'

Vincent took her hand to lead her through the crush. They pushed along for a yard or so, then saw a clearer path ahead. A tall, powerful figure was cutting an easier passage for those behind him. With a premonition of fear, Crystal recognised the broad shoulders and dark, curly head of Dan Farraday! She tried to turn back, but the crowd behind pushed her on.

'Nearly there,' Vincent said. 'And see who's ahead? It's Dan Farraday. I thought he'd gone to the States.'

Crystal pulled away, too late. Dan Farraday had seen her, his eyebrows shooting up in surprise.

'Crystal Tempest! How you dog my footsteps. Work or play. Don't you ever give up?'

'What? You don't think I came here because . . . you . . . I'd no idea you'd be here. It's ridiculous. Vincent said you were away. How could you imagine I'd want to see you anywhere but where I have to . . . on the site?'

'Ah, Vincent, too. And with you? Well, well.'

A scowl darkened his attractive face.

'Having conveniently disposed of poor Neville once you'd landed the Brinscombe job, you're scalp-collecting again. I'm afraid Vincent won't mind me saying, he doesn't yet have the same sort of clout as a Drummond, or is it some other devious game you're playing?'

His eyes narrowed, but Crystal saw hostility and suspicion in their depths.

'I wonder exactly what you're up to?' he continued.

'You've no right to speak to me like that,' she lashed out. 'What I do is none of your business, and if I'd known you'd be here tonight I probably wouldn't have come at all.'

'I'm surprised you were invited, after dumping Sir Richard's son.'

'Don't dare assume anything.' Crystal's eyes flashed fury.

'I'm afraid I don't know what's going on here,' Vincent interrupted.

A small, fragile-looking girl with fluffy blonde hair put her hand on Dan's sleeve.

'Dan, either introduce me to your friends, or let's eat. I'm starving.'

He patted the delicate, soft, pearl-tipped fingers.

'OK, I'm sorry, it's just . . . '

He shook his head, glared at Crystal and said unceremoniously, 'Alicia, this is Vincent Wain, from the practice, and Crystal Tempest, a site worker. Now let's find some food.'

He took the girl's arm and turned away, his dismissive disdain riling Crystal to rage.

'You . . . ! You . . . I can't stand another minute!'

She suddenly broke off, aware of a change in the rhythm of the party noise. The random babble changed to shock-waves of alarm, spinning outwards from the entrance to the dining-room. She sensed panic, dismay, heard snatches on a higher decibel.

'Collapsed . . . who . . . is there a doctor?'

Everyone craned to see, moving to the centre of the disturbance, then her blood drained as she heard, 'It's Sir Richard!'

She pushed, shoved, but could get nowhere.

102

'Let me through, please.'

In a minute, someone would get hurt. She looked up as crowds were pressed against the curving staircase, some struggling to get away.

'Everyone, stay still, where you are. Sir Richard's been taken ill. He needs air, and a clear passageway for help. A doctor's trying to come through. Someone back there, call an ambulance.'

The clear ringing tone of authority quietened the panic and people began to move slowly and sensibly away from the dining-room. Dan Farraday, head and shoulders above the rest, calmly marshalled the crowd and a clear way miraculously melted. A man hurried through.

'I'm a doctor.'

Crystal darted forward to follow him, but found her shoulder roughly seized as she was flung back.

'Get away, you little fool. The man's sick. There's nothing to see.'

She twisted violently, out of the

hateful grasp, and struck his hand from her shoulder.

'Get off! Don't dare touch me. I've got to get to him.'

'You . . . monster. Can't you understand? Sir Richard is seriously ill. He's collapsed.'

He gripped her arm as she spat out, 'He's my uncle, you . . . you damned, bossy idiot.'

For a split second, the tension of his grip changed, then, still grasping her arm, he followed the doctor, pulling Crystal along with him.

6

Cold fear struck Crystal as she kneeled by Dick Drummond's prone body. She touched his hand, to discover it was clammy cold. His breathing was hoarsely laboured. The doctor looked across at her.

'You are?'

'His niece, Crystal Tempest. How bad is it?'

'Not good, I'm afraid. Looks like a pretty severe heart attack. Someone's rung for an ambulance. If we can get him to hospital quickly, there's a chance. There's no Lady Drummond?'

'No. Aunt Elspeth died fifteen years ago. Neville, his son, is here, or was. He'll be back . . . please . . . he looks so dreadful. Can't you do something?'

The doctor shook his head.

'Not until the ambulance arrives. It

shouldn't be long. They know it's an emergency.'

Crystal clasped her hands together in agony.

'I can't bear to see him like this.'

Dick's eyes were open, and he tried to speak to her.

'No, Uncle Dick, rest. Stay quiet.'

Dan Farraday kneeled beside her, touched her shoulders. Dick's eyes flickered to Dan and closed as he attempted a smile.

In spite of her gripping anxiety, Crystal registered the concern in Dan's eyes. It made him look softer, younger — the granite exterior usually on display every time they met was in abeyance. She looked round.

'I must find Neville. He's gone to take Carla home and . . .'

'I'll wait here for him, unless you'd like me to come in the ambulance.'

She shook her head.

Dan stood up.

'I'll go and see if there's any sign of it.' Then he was gone, shouldering his way through the guests.

Crystal turned back to her uncle, took his hand, pressed it, trying to warm it in both of hers. Minutes later, the paramedics arrived. Working at high speed, they administered oxygen, put up a drip, and in no time her uncle was strapped to a stretcher and on his way to the ambulance, drawn up close to the front entrance. Crystal kept as near to her uncle as possible.

'Please, please, Uncle Dick, don't die!' she breathed in prayer.

She saw Vincent's anxious face in the watching crowd. He came forward.

'Crystal, is there anything I can do?'

'No, no. I'm sorry.' Distracted, her eyes sought for Dan who was by the ambulance door. 'Neville?'

Dan shook his head.

'Not here yet. Don't worry, I'll find him.'

His reassuring smile was the last thing she saw before the ambulance doors closed and they were off, lights flashing and sirens blaring, through the busy London streets.

The paramedics were monitoring every laboured breath and heartbeat.

'He'll be all right?'

'Couldn't say, miss. He'll be in intensive care within minutes.'

His companion spoke urgently on the radio to warn the hospital of their arrival time.

'There'll be a team standing by.'

'He's always been so fit, never an illness that I know of.'

She desperately needed to hear comfort, but none was forthcoming.

'Doesn't always follow. Sir Dick Drummond, isn't it? Boss of Drummond Construction? Pretty stressful job ... 'specially these days ... here we are, miss.'

A team of doctors and nurses took charge, and Crystal ran with them along what seemed an interminable length of corridor, through a pair of double doors, where she found herself politely but firmly barred from following her uncle into the intensive care unit.

'Can't I come, too?'

She felt scared that if she left her uncle's side for a minute, he'd be cut off from the vitality she was willing into him.

'Nothing you can do. Now, we'll take good care of him. Someone'll come as soon as there's any news. There's a waiting-room just down there, and a drinks machine along the corridor.'

With a quick, professional smile, the nurse was gone.

Crystal was halfway through her second cup of bitter-tasting coffee when Neville came running down the corridor, followed by Dan Farraday.

'Neville! Thank goodness!' Crystal cried.

'Dad?'

'No news yet. It's been an age. I can't find anyone to ask.'

'I'll see,' Dan volunteered.

'They took him through there, but they wouldn't let me through.'

Dan pushed his way through the banned doors.

Crystal put her arms around Neville. 'I'm so sorry. I can't believe it. Uncle Dick! Always so tough . . . so durable!'

'I should have seen it coming. He's been working every hour God sends just lately. I've hardly seen him. I should've noticed. He was so irritable. I thought it was me!' Neville's voice was trembling as he spoke.

'You're not to blame. I love him dearly, but he's not the easiest man to tell what to do.'

'I've just been too wrapped up in my own concerns, whining on about how I disliked working at Drummond's. That can't have helped Dad's condition.'

'You weren't to know,' Crystal comforted.

'I should have known. There is one bright spot. He really took to Carla, even asked us out for a meal next week. Oh, Crystal, what'll I do if . . . if . . . '

'Don't even think about it. You'll just have to postpone things until he's

110

better, and when he is better, we must take more care of him.'

'No need to tell me — if only we get the chance. Here's Dan. He's been great. What did you find out?'

Dan looked grim.

'Not the best news I'm afraid. A massive heart attack. You didn't know he's been seeing a consultant for over a year?'

'No! Why didn't he tell me?'

'Never told anyone, but the point is, he was advised to slack off the work pace. Of course, he wouldn't. They're in there fighting, but it is a fight, for his life.'

'I must go to him.'

Neville moved towards the door.

'They'll let you see him for a few seconds,' Dan said. 'He's heavily sedated, and he looks terrible. Be prepared, he's attached to a mass of wires and tubes.'

'I don't mind that. I just want to see him.'

'It's just through those doors . . . no,

not you, Crystal. They're adamant. Only his son — no other visitors.'

'I'm not a visitor! I'm his niece.'

'All the same, let Neville go alone.'

He laid a hand on her arm, and they waited silently, side by side in the corridor, so quiet and tranquil it was hard to believe only yards away her beloved uncle was fighting for his very existence.

Neville came back, stunned.

'Dad looks so helpless, wired up to all those things. How he'd hate it if he knew what was going on. They're only giving him a fifty-fifty chance at best. He's not stabilised.'

He sat down and buried his head in his hands.

'Neville, I'm so sorry.'

Crystal put her arms round him again.

'I'll stay with you.'

After a few minutes, he looked up.

'No, I'd rather be alone. And there's Carla. This is her hospital, you know. She works on Surgical. I'll ring her just before she comes on shift. It'll be good to know she's nearby. Dan, could you run Crystal home? It's awfully late.'

'I'd rather stay and I can take a taxi,' Crystal insisted.

'Go home and get some rest. I might need you tomorrow. Please, Crystal.'

'I should ring Mum in Spain. She's his sister, after all,' she explained to Dan.

'Best leave it until morning. She's enough to worry her with Uncle Jack,' Neville said.

'She'd never forgive me, if . . . '

Dan said gently, 'If the worst does happen, your mother couldn't get here in time, and if Dick comes out of this, tomorrow will be time enough.'

A few hours earlier, Crystal would have told him to mind his own business. Now she simply nodded.

'All right, but there's no need for you to bother taking me home.'

'No bother.'

He extended a hand to Neville.

'Good luck. I'll keep in touch, and

believe me, your father's a survivor. He'll come through.'

'Thanks for all your help tonight.'

Crystal could see her cousin's attention was beyond the double doors with his father, and with one backward glance, she allowed herself to be led away. The red Porsche was blatantly and illegally parked by the hospital entrance. Dan opened the passenger door.

'You see,' he murmured, 'it's as good as new — almost.'

Crystal blushed. The memory of their first encounter seemed somehow inappropriate now. She gave him her address, settled back in the luxury of the leather seat, then shot bolt upright.

'What about the girl you came to the party with? Alicia?'

Dan spun the car out of the hospital grounds and into the street.

'Alicia? She's been taken good care of. She'll understand.'

Traffic at the pre-dawn hour was light as they swished along softly.

Crystal looked at Dan's profile, strongly outlined in the passing lights. His hands on the wheel were sure and steady as he turned to meet her glance. She looked away, confused.

'Try not to worry about your uncle. He's tough.'

'So I keep telling myself. I wish I could believe it.'

'Why didn't you tell me you were related?'

'I should have thought that was obvious. I'm not proud of the fact that I had to beg him for a chance at Drummond's. He hates family working in the firm. Keeping the fact he was my uncle secret was his condition of employment, and one I preferred anyway.'

'Neville works at Drummond's.'

'Uncle Dick's convinced that that's a mistake, and he has other personal reasons.' She leaned back wearily. 'Neville and I both feel so guilty. We never noticed he was overworking. Why was he? He didn't need to . . .'

Dan was silent for a while, then he said flatly, 'You don't know?'

'Know what?'

'Drummond's isn't doing too well at the moment.'

'Not what? But Uncle Dick's always so positive, so optimistic. I thought business was booming.'

'It was, but lately . . . ' He hesitated. 'I suppose I can trust you, now I know you're his niece. At one point I suspected that perhaps you were part of it, but obviously, as you're his family, I was wrong.'

'Suspected me as part of what? What are you talking about? Tell me.'

'Dick's tried to keep things quiet. One hint of trouble, especially in the construction business, and you're dead!'

'Trouble? But there's lots of work in. There's Brinscombe, European projects . . . '

'Ah, there's the nub of it. There's a huge Euro-Consortium, desperate to swallow up Drummond's. Your uncle's

116

dead against it, but to withstand that sort of pressure on shareholders you've got to be in a strong, solvent position. Drummond's isn't. Several things have gone wrong in the past twelve months. Drummond's tenders have been undercut, apparent breaches of safety regulations . . . '

'Dick wouldn't do such a thing. He's paranoid about safety!'

'He may be, but he can't be everywhere. He has to rely on his managers. There's something fishy going on. Faulty materials turn up . . . '

Crystal remembered the suspect planking at Brinscombe Manor. It had seemed odd at the time. She decided not to mention it until she'd investigated a bit further.

'That late start clause from Brinscombe Manor was a cash-flow problem. Dick admitted it to me, in the strictest confidence. That mustn't get out, and now his heart attack'll put the City into jitters. There's no-one at Drummond's strong enough to take Dick's place. If it all falls apart . . . '

'What about Neville?' Crystal interrupted but Dan was quick to respond.

'Hasn't exactly proved a pillar of strength yet. Drummond's can't afford to display any sort of weakness, hint of disaster, or scandal. What do you think tonight's party was all about?'

'Uncle Dick often gives parties.'

'Not as lavish as tonight's. Everyone of any importance in the trade was there — and more. It was his show of strength — money no object and Drummond's doing fine — no worries! It may have worked, but for the heart attack. Everyone there saw Dick Drummond carried out unconscious on a stretcher — a bad image for a firm fighting for survival.

'He's done a fine job keeping going, but at a great cost to his health. And he has managed to keep his troubles secret, though I don't know how. One other thing — the slightest smear in any way connected to his business, and that'd be it. Drummond's would be over the edge, delivered into the hands of the Euro-Consortium, which would immediately get rid of Sir Richard for their own man. Drummond's, as we know it, would be finished.'

Crystal felt sick. With a dreadful sense of foreboding she could see what lay in the future. The arrival of the news she dreaded from America and the subsequent publicity over her and her connection with Drummond's, the very fact that she was working for the firm, surely would be enough to administer the final blow to the firm.

7

As Crystal let herself into her apartment, the phone rang. It was four-thirty in the morning. Who could it be? She picked it up uneasily.

'Crystal, it's me, Mum. I'm sorry to be ringing at this hour, but I've been worried sick. I phoned Dick to wish him a happy birthday and got a garbled account about him being rushed to hospital. I've been ringing you every half hour.'

'Oh, Mum! He's had a heart attack. It's serious. I was going to ring you.'

'I'll get the first plane out,' her mother interrupted. 'Which hospital? I'll meet you there. No, I'll get a taxi from Heathrow, to save time. I'll have to go now, no time to lose. 'Bye, love, and try not to worry. I'll see you later, and remember, Uncle Dick's a survivor.'

Crystal, thankful for her mother's brisk, practical competence, hoped Uncle Dick had the strength everyone assumed he possessed.

Noon on Sunday saw Sir Richard Drummond still fighting, but by the most slender of threads. The consultant at the hospital could give no assurances. Crystal was allowed to see her uncle briefly but he was so hemmed in by apparatus and nurses she was almost too scared to touch him. She held his hand and talked quietly for a while.

He raised a smile, tiredly said her name, but her uncle had little strength left for anything more. It was only when Crystal saw her mother sweep into the ward like a breath of air that she and Neville managed to cheer up a little.

Helen Tempest hugged both daughter and nephew, then frowned, her eyes stern.

'For goodness' sake! If Dick sees you two, he'll give up the struggle straight away and send for the undertaker.

Dick's not going to die! He's too precious.'

'Mum, he's really very ill,' Crystal whispered, fighting back tears.

'I know that,' Helen said quietly, 'but we shan't let him go. I've brought your father through things as bad as this. Now, Neville, you look appalling. Go home and get some sleep. Crystal, you don't look much better, and there's a most attractive man waiting for you downstairs. I approve wholeheartedly. He's going to take you out of here for a while.'

'Who?'

'Dan Farraday, he said. Isn't he that architect whose car you said you'd smashed up? Good choice of target, dear. He doesn't seem to bear you any grudge.'

'Mum, you're outrageous! He's just being kind. He knows Uncle Dick, through business.'

'All the better. Now shoo. I'm going to talk to the consultant.'

'You're sure it's all right to go?'

Crystal was reluctant, but it would be wonderful to get away from the hospital for a while. The sight of Uncle Dick so weak and helpless haunted her.

'I'm sure,' Helen replied. 'And Neville's nearly asleep on his feet anyway. I guarantee, nothing dreadful will happen to Dick while I'm around. Your father sends his love, by the way. He's much better. Now, go! I'm going to be busy. Sister's making coffee for me.'

Crystal's heart gave a little flip when she saw Dan lounging in a chair in the reception area, surrounded by a mountain of newspapers. His dark sweater was the same blue as his eyes — and they looked stormy!

'Crystal,' he said as he got to his feet, 'how is he?'

She spread her hands forlornly. 'No better, but Mum says he'll pull through.'

'Yes, I met her. We both arrived together. She's unmistakable, you look so like her. I hope she hasn't had a chance to read these, and I hope Dick doesn't see them.'

He jabbed viciously at the newspapers.

'Someone's behind this . . . this . . . smear campaign.'

He folded back a page in the business section of a leading Sunday broadsheet. Bold headlines leaped out at Crystal.

Drummond's To Topple. Top Executive Has Heart Attack at Birthday Party.

Quickly, she scanned the columns and phrases jumped out at her.

The final straw for Drummond's . . . demise of leading construction company possible now the life of Sir Richard . . .

There were hints of further revelations to come in a fuller report. She flung the paper down.

'What's going on? How did all this happen so quickly? All these innuendoes, nothing concrete.'

'That's the problem. There is nothing yet, but you can bet your life that within the next few days, they'll dredge up something disreputable about the firm, and if there's nothing, well, they'll make it up! This is just the beginning.'

'Dan, you don't think . . . it seems crazy but . . . '

She told him then about the faulty timber.

'Possible. It could be just a coincidence. I'll come to the site first thing tomorrow and see for myself. You took the timber out, I hope.'

'Of course.'

'Good girl!' He scrunched up the newspapers and stuffed them into a litter bin. 'And now, I'm going to take you out to lunch. It's a lovely day. We'll take a walk by the river and forget all about Drummond's for an hour or so.'

'I don't think I'm very hungry.'

'Of course you are! If you're not, I'll eat for both of us. I know just the place.'

He did — of course! He would, wouldn't he, Crystal thought, as she leaned back against the sun-warmed wall of the small pub tucked away down a side alley. It boasted a tiny garden, so secluded and shaded with bushes, it was hard to believe they were in the heart of London.

Dan had led her on a leisurely stroll by the Thames. He'd kept the conversation light and impersonal, pointed out landmarks, chatted about the City, theatre, concerts, exhibitions.

He held her hand as they walked, and it seemed a natural thing to do. Gradually she grew calmer, and by the time they reached the pub garden, she found that indeed she was quite hungry!

'Told you,' he said smugly, as she reached for a fourth smoked-salmon sandwich. 'Have more wine. It'll help you relax.'

'I am relaxed. Just half a glass. It's lovely, thank you.'

They were sitting side-by-side on a rough, wooden bench, his arm casually spread along the back, very close to her, but not touching. He wore dark glasses against the strong sunlight, so Crystal couldn't fathom his expression, but he appeared to be studying her intently. Lazily he dropped his hand to her shoulder.

'You know, Crystal, you're an intriguing sort of girl. That day you tried to run me over . . . '

'I didn't . . . '

'That day,' he continued, ignoring her protest, 'you were a spitting harpy, a female fury, and later, at the clients' meeting, you were a tornado! Today, you're as soft and gentle as . . . as a zephyr. I wonder, which is the real Crystal Tempest.'

Very lightly, he touched her cheek, running his finger down to her mouth. It lingered there a moment while she held very still, hardly daring to breathe.

'Do you have a persona you keep especially for work, or has your uncle's heart attack weakened your defences? What are you scared of in your working life, Crystal?'

The moment held. There was no-one

else in the garden. Dan took off his sun glasses and looked directly into her eyes. She stared back, mesmerised.

'Can I get you anything else, sir?'

A young man had appeared and picked up the empty wine bottle. He wiped the surface of the table. Dan replaced his glasses.

'No, no thanks, unless, Crystal . . . ?'

She shook her head, and the waiter went away. They leaned back companionably. She closed her eyes to the sun.

'I'm not scared of anything, but I would like to know something. Why do you hate women in the profession?'

Dan didn't answer for a while, and Crystal felt a barely perceptible movement of his body away from her.

'It's a tough world. Women are too emotional.'

'That's not fair, and a terrible generalisation,' she said angrily.

'You prove my point. Your reaction just then is entirely emotional.'

'But we're not at work now. It's just a

point of discussion. There are so many good women engineers and surveyors.'

'Then I've yet to meet them — excluding you, of course. I have to admit you're doing a good job at Brinscombe Manor. What I especially appreciate is you are able to follow my instructions, to the letter.'

She persisted.

'You haven't explained what you have against women in the construction industry.'

He stood up.

'I don't have to explain to you. My reasons are personal and private. Now I think we'd best be getting back to see how your uncle is.'

The spell was broken. Slowly she followed him out of the garden. He drove back to the hospital, where they found Helen and Neville still there. Crystal realised guiltily she'd actually forgotten about her uncle for minutes at a time whilst she'd been out with Dan.

'You look a lot better,' her mother

greeted her. 'Your young man has done a good job.'

She smiled at Dan.

'Mother! He's not my young man,' Crystal whispered in embarrassment.

'Ah, well. I can still ask him another favour though?'

'Anything you like, Helen.'

Crystal thought Dan was all too eager to fall under her mother's spell!

'I want to stay here a while longer, so could I borrow your car, Crystal? I wondered if Dan could drop you off at your flat.'

'Mother, I can get the Tube, or wait with you.'

'No. I've asked the consultant. Dick's no worse, no better, but I want to sit by him. He knows I'm here, and it'll help him fight. Please, Crystal, that's what I came for, to help my brother.'

'Of course.'

Crystal kissed her mother and handed over the car keys.

'You'll come to the flat later?' she asked.

'If all goes well here. I'll ring you. Thank you so much, Dan, for taking Crystal out today.'

'It wasn't much of a problem,' he said gravely, but his tone irritated Crystal.

They drove back from the hospital in silence. She was beginning to feel jumpy but she put it down to being tired and the sun and wine had made her sleepy. She almost dozed off in the car, and came to a start as Dan stopped outside the entrance to her apartment building.

'Pretty impressive address you've got, Miss Tempest.'

'Would you like to come up for a coffee?' she asked, sure he'd refuse.

'Yes, please. Coffee would be good.'

She punched the numbers of the security system, wishing he wouldn't stand so closely behind her. Once inside her flat, she felt even more uneasy, as he prowled around the huge sitting-room, looking at the pictures, taking in the expensive leather sofas and exquisite

131

Chinese silk carpets.

'Please, sit down. I'll put on the coffee.'

But he followed her into the streamlined, beautifully-equipped kitchen. She fumbled as she measured out coffee into the filter.

'Very impressive. You must be doing very well to be able to afford this, unless, of course, you share it with some very rich partner.'

'It's none of your business,' Crystal snapped, turning on the tap with such force, the water hit the sink bowl and splashed straight back at her.

She was drenched. Angrily, she shook back her hair. What on earth was the matter with her?

'Here, allow me.'

Dan picked up a towel and started to mop up the drips on her arm. She snatched the towel from him, her heart pounding like a mad thing.

'Hey, Crystal, take it easy.'

He put his arms round her.

'Am I making you nervous? You're

still worrying about Dick. Look, he'll be all right. Why, you're shaking.'

Crystal would have given anything to stop that tell-tale trembling. She shut her eyes and took a deep breath. Still her wretched legs wobbled like jelly. She daren't move out of the circle of his arms in case she fell over.

'I'm just . . . just a bit tired — reaction I expect, too.'

He stroked back her hair, flicking the wet spots off her cheek.

'Not surprising. Forget the coffee. You've had a dreadful shock. It's time you got some sleep.'

He pulled her closer to him, one hand cradling her head into his shoulder.

'Poor Crystal,' he murmured, 'you're not such a tough cookie as you try to make out. Crystal-sharp on the outside, butter-soft inside.'

He released her head and tilted back her face so that her honey hair rippled down over her shoulders.

She watched his mouth, soft and

133

sensuous, no longer the hard line she'd seen so many times, and nothing in the world could stop her own lips parting as his came down to meet them. For seconds he held her gently, then drew her so hard to him she gasped, automatically sliding her arms round him in response.

It seemed to her that all the bells in London were ringing in her ears. The sensation of Dan's body, moulded to hers, was incredibly heady. Never in her life before, not even with Dwight, had she wanted this to go on and on for ever. To her shame, when she remembered afterwards, it was Dan who pulled away first, his dark eyes dazed, then frowning.

'I . . . I didn't need to do that.'

He stepped right away from her and took his car keys out of his pocket.

'I'll go,' he said abruptly. 'You need to rest.'

His eyes swept around the apartment in one last puzzled look. He nodded briefly to Crystal, and left.

She stood motionless, hands pressed against her mouth. What an absolute idiot she'd been! Hadn't her experience in the States taught her anything? Never, she'd vowed then, never again would she mix business with pleasure. But then, she'd never experienced that sort of pleasure before!

She groaned aloud. Dan Farraday was visiting Brinscombe Manor first thing in the morning. She closed her eyes. How on earth could she face him? That kiss — by no stretch of the imagination had it been a friendly good-evening, we've-had-a-nice-day-out sort of kiss. Or perhaps Dan Farraday kissed all the women he spent time with like that! She remembered Alicia . . .

8

Crystal set her alarm for an early start Monday morning. She had to face Dan, but at least she wouldn't give him the satisfaction of being late. Just after the alarm rang, her mother returned from the hospital.

'Mum! You must be shattered. What's the news?'

'Holding his own, thank goodness, and marginally improved. The cardiologist was prepared to be a bit hopeful. That's why I'm here, to snatch a bit of sleep. What a beautiful flat, Crystal. Weren't you lucky Tim pushed off to New Zealand?'

'Yes. Mum, I must dash. Make yourself at home. I daren't be late for work. Dan Farraday's making a special site inspection this morning.'

Her mother yawned.

'That'll be nice, darling,' she said sleepily.

'No, I don't think it will but there's nothing I can do about it. Oh, and Mum, make sure Uncle Dick doesn't see any Sunday papers.'

'I've already seen to that.'

'Dan thinks there's something more sinister behind it. We'll talk tonight.'

A quick hug and she was gone. The faster she got to work the sooner the morning would be over!

She was right — it wasn't a nice visit. Dan Farraday, she decided, was the perfect example of Dr Jekyll and Mr Hyde. Yesterday, charming, caring Dr Jekyll. Monday morning, at his most snarling Mr Hyde. He inspected the timbers, declared them flawed, demanded that one particular house be reroofed, and gave them all a thorough rollicking for not noticing it before.

Even Jim Reynolds, usually as stolid and unemotional as a rock, shifted uneasily from foot to foot as his competence as a manager was called into question.

'I suppose no-one thought to check the timber merchants?'

Dan glared angrily round the cramped site office, where both Vincent and Crystal were trying to assume a nonchalance neither felt.

'I did, actually,' Crystal ventured, trying desperately to shut out that image of Dan, the man who'd kissed her only hours ago! 'They swore there was nothing wrong with the timber they dispatched.' Her tone was icy.

'Did you go and see for yourself?'

'Er . . . well, no . . . but I will.'

'Don't bother, I'll see to it myself. Seems the only way to get efficiency round here is to do the job myself. I don't want anything like this occurring again. Each of you, Jim, Crystal, Vincent, will check the quality of every piece of equipment that goes into every single building. Got it?'

They all nodded dejectedly but they knew he was right.

'I still don't understand.' Jim shook his head. 'Why would anyone slip us faulty timbers?'

'Slow down the whole process. You're well ahead of schedule. That might not be popular in some quarters. If Crystal hadn't spotted that first bit of roofing, you'd have had to rip off all the roofs in that housing section. That would have put your schedule way off course.'

'Glad I did something right,' Crystal muttered.

He shot her a dark look.

'Miss Tempest, anything else?' he queried.

'There is one thing I meant to mention. Those tiles for the bathrooms.'

'Yes?' he barked at her. 'Nothing wrong there, I hope. I selected them myself in Italy.'

'No, they're lovely to look at, but they're not non-slip. They'll be dangerous.'

'Of course, they're non-slip. Do you think I'd contemplate any other kind?'

'But they aren't. When I was in the

States, there was a building firm who'd used them, and a lady who bought one of the apartments slipped, broke her hip, and sued the company. I don't think we should use those tiles.'

Everyone held their breath. There was not a sound in the site office, and there was the darkest frown she'd ever seen on Dan's face, apart from when he'd crashed the Porsche into the JCB.

It wasn't so much an explosion as an icy blast when he spoke.

'Your job is to carry out the specifications on the plans. No more, no less. Your experience in America is irrelevant here. Just do as you're told. Let me worry about the consequences of my judgement.'

'Phew!' Jim said when Dan and Vincent had gone. 'What was all that about?'

Crystal shrugged.

'Bear with a sore head this morning. Let's hope that's his last visit for a bit!'

News of Sir Richard's illness had buzzed round the site first thing, and

Crystal realised it was going to be impossible to keep their relationship secret any longer, especially as she needed time to visit the hospital. Her news made a few waves. Everyone on site was sympathetic, but more concerned about the rumour about Drummond's. These men's jobs were on the line and the firm's long-standing employees were puzzled and furious over the implications that Drummond's was a sinking ship.

The good news over the next few days was that by the end of the week Sir Richard had turned the corner and was on the road back to recovery. But he was still banned by his consultant from even mentioning work to Neville or Crystal, and as things were, they were only too thankful for that restriction.

At the end of the second week, Helen came to say goodbye to her brother. Neville and Crystal were to drive her to Heathrow.

'Now, Richard, don't ever scare us like that again.'

She kissed him fondly.

'I'm going to be keeping a stricter eye on you in future. The consultant says you're to come out to us in Spain the minute you're out of hospital. All mention of business will be banned!'

Dick eased back on his pillows, still very tired by every movement.

'Don't worry, I promise I'll take it easy. Neville seems to be doing all right, from what I've been allowed to hear.'

'He's been quite remarkable,' Crystal confirmed. 'Honest, Uncle, you won't be needed at all at this rate!'

'Little Carla sees me every day, too. I'm hoping I'll have something to get really fit for soon.'

He winked knowingly at Neville.

'I hope so, too, Dad, as soon as you're strong enough. I've arranged for you to fly straight to Spain from hospital.'

'That's a bit drastic. I'd like to pop home for a day or two first.'

'It's what the doctor ordered,' Neville lied.

'Well, it was only a half truth,' he said to Crystal, coming back from seeing Helen off. 'A conspiracy more like. Dad mustn't get an inkling of what's going on at Drummond's, not until he's much stronger. The doctors are all agreeing. Spain was a brilliant idea of Aunt Helen's.'

'It's the only way we can stop him reading the papers. There's a bit of a lull at the moment.'

'Bad news, though. We lost that contract for the leisure complex in Scotland.'

'No! I thought it was all signed and sealed.'

'So did I, but they pulled out. A cheaper tender apparently, though how anyone could undercut the price we gave, I'll never know.'

'Oh, Neville, I'm really sorry. You put a lot of work in there.'

'Can't be helped. And in a strange way I'm enjoying work, for the first time ever at Drummond's.'

'That's because you're in charge,

making all the decisions.'

'I just hope I get them right, that's all. How's Brinscombe Manor coming along?'

She held up crossed fingers.

'Fine, so far. The first houses will be completed next week. Cash should be flowing in. Anything else I can do to help, apart from Brinscombe?'

'I'd like to talk over one or two things, use you as a sounding board perhaps?'

'Any time, you know that.'

Neville's call for help came sooner than either of them expected. The next day, Crystal was late home from work. It had been a difficult day, morale was low because of the uncertainties of Drummond's future, and the work pace had slowed. Crystal could see the precious days ahead of schedule slipping away. She had to think of some way of revitalising the work-force. Maybe Jim would agree to some sort of special bonus incentive.

She took note-pad and pencil, a plate

of sandwiches and a glass of wine into the sitting-room for a working supper. She flicked on the nine o'clock news, turned the sound down, and started on some figures. As she worked away, she glanced up at odd moments to catch sight of one or two news items as they come up on the screen. Then one particular scene made her freeze. She reached for the remote control and turned up the sound.

The screen showed the aftermath of some sort of explosion, men working furiously to clear debris and rubble. She closed her eyes. It couldn't be! But the dumper trucks in the shot were unmistakable, almost larger than life. DRUMMOND'S, she could read in black and fluorescent orange. She adjusted the sound as the picture returned to the announcer. Then there was a map on the screen — Spain!

A tunnel connecting two new stretches of motorway cut through a mountainous region. Vaguely she recalled Neville talking about it. It had started over a year ago, and was now nearing completion. She'd heard talk that Uncle Dick was planning a ceremonial opening and Helen had agreed to be hostess at a grand party.

The TV announcer looked grave.

'Worst accident of its kind in that part of Spain. One man has been killed, with the possibility of many more injuries to come. There are several more workers still trapped in the tunnel, and fears are growing for their lives. It is understood that an on-the-spot worker complained that safety procedures on the site were not as stringent as they could be. The explosion is one of a series of incidents within the troubled construction company giant, Drummond's Limited whose shares hit an all-time low last week following allegations of shoddy workmanship in one of Drummond's prestigious retirement complexes. Sir Richard Drummond is currently in a London hospital recovering from a heart attack . . . '

Crystal switched off the set. She

didn't want to hear any more. Just as she did so, the phone rang.

'Crystal? Neville here. You've heard?'

'Just seen the news. It's dreadful. Uncle Dick — will he know?'

'Won't have seen it with any luck. I went over this evening. He's making good progress, talking about being out and about soon, but TV's still banned, on my orders. But he's beginning to suspect something's up. Sooner or later someone's bound to say something. I'll try to get him out to Aunt Helen's.'

'Is that wise in the circumstances? The accident was in Spain!'

'Other side of the country from the villa. Look, Crystal, I've now got to go to Spain myself, with our Chief Engineer. All this about poor safety regulations is rubbish. We've got Jack Anderson over there in charge. He's an absolute stickler for safety. We're flying out in an hour. Can you keep an eye on Dad? Use your discretion. Tell him anything you like, but get him off to Aunt Helen's as soon as possible.'

'I'll try. I just can't believe what's happening.'

'I can, and I'm beginning to believe Dan's theory. Drummond's shares will slide even lower tomorrow. I'll be back as soon as I can. Thanks, Crystal, and, oh, if you've time, could you ring Carla for me. Explain I couldn't reach her.'

Next day's newspaper carried front-page pictures of the tunnel explosion. The story about safety had been picked up by several tabloids.

At the Brinscombe Manor site, Crystal was aware of uneasy glances from the men, sympathetic looks. The atmosphere was gloomy but she put that down to the horror of the accident. Although the main work force at the tunnel had been Spanish, there was British labour out there as well. They would all be thinking the same — it could've been them in that tunnel.

Jim came into the office at midday, holding a newspaper as though it was red hot.

'Crystal, you'd better see this. I'm

very concerned your uncle doesn't get hold of it. It involves your family, too.'

She took it gingerly. There, on a full middle-page spread, was a screaming banner headline.

Workers' Lives for Boss's Profits.

It was far worse than anything she'd seen so far. It stopped just short of downright accusation that Drummond's had flagrantly ignored safety requirements on many of their sites, and went on to recount several stories of workers' injuries.

'Jim, this is crazy. Even with perfect safety procedures there's bound to be some accidents. These are probably all documented in the files. Hang on, where would this rag have got hold of all this stuff?'

'Pretty easy. Just careful research, or a bit of inside information, and the piece on your dad, well, that was well covered at the time . . . '

'Dad!'

'Afraid so. All that about your

father's accident has been dragged up, with the implication that even your uncle's own brother-in-law was a victim. I'm sorry, Crystal. It must be very painful.'

'Sir Richard has never stopped blaming himself for Dad's accident, and it wasn't even his fault, but it'll certainly kill him if he sees this.'

'Anything I can do?' Jim asked anxiously.

'I could at least phone the hospital, to warn them, but I daren't go there. He'd suspect, especially if I'm supposed to be at work. I'm just not sure what to do.'

They both looked up at the screech of tyres. The familiar red Porsche had scorched to a stop feet away from them. Dan Farraday, face black as spades, stormed out, slamming the door behind him.

'Jim! Crystal!'

'It's our midday break.'

Crystal was suddenly conscious that both she and her manager were standing around apparently chatting idly.

'I understand. What do you think I am? Jim, I'm taking Crystal off for the rest of the day. Can you manage?'

'Well, sure, if I have to.'

'You do. This is an emergency. You've seen it, too?'

He glowered at the offending paper, still clutched in Crystal's hand.

'Garbage,' he said crisply, took it from her, screwed it up and tossed it in the bin. 'Unfortunately for Drummond's though that sort of garbage can do a lot of damage. Come on Crystal, back to London. We've a plane to catch.'

'What?'

'Get in. No time to waste.'

He bundled her into the car, gave a perfunctory wave to Jim, and roared off.

'Dan, please, where are we going?'

'I told you. A plane — Heathrow.'

'But I can't go!'

'We're not going anywhere. Too

much to do here scotching all these vicious rumours. I've already got my lawyers on it.'

'But . . . '

'If you keep quiet instead of squeaking I'll explain. All this nonsense will put your uncle right back where he started from, and worse, it's making me burst blood vessels!'

'I had noticed . . . sorry.'

'So Dick has to be got out of the way. Neville phoned me before he left for Spain. I was going to ring you but events have forced the pace a bit. A friend of mine has a private jet, and he's very happy to fly Sir Richard out to Spain tonight. Helen's got everything ready at her end. The villa's tucked away in the hills and she'll be able to monitor the news. From what she told me it's pretty remote there.'

'Won't the tunnel accident be the hottest news out there though?'

'That's a bit of a problem, but with any luck we'll be able to clear Drummond's of any negligence in a few days' time. The hospital's already surrounded by reporters, but if it's a natural disaster the firm won't be blamed.'

'But mud will stick, especially after all the other things.'

Dan took his hand off the wheel and briefly stroked her hair.

'It's all so diabolical, unpardonable, but I think I'm beginning to see the daylight in all this.'

'Dan! What?'

'You'll know soon enough, if I'm right. Now, all you have to do is to act natural with your uncle. I've briefed the medical staff and had a long talk with Dick this morning before I came to pick you up. I've almost persuaded him your mother's so worried about him being in London, she's about to abandon Jack to come back here. The only way to stop her coming is for him to go to Spain himself so she can keep an eye on both brother and husband.'

'Genius. You're a born fixer.'

'We'll tell Dick I'm entirely responsible for taking you off the job for an hour or two to see him off.'

'You've thought of everything.'

'Just one more thing. Once we've seen Dick safely away from all this, I'm taking you to dinner.'

'I can't, unless I go back to the flat first.'

She looked down at her work clothes.

'Don't bother. We're not going anywhere where it matters what you wear. Here's the terminal entrance so put your best actress foot forward.'

'Dan, why are you going to all this trouble for my uncle?'

He slowed down, followed the short-term parking signs and stopped the car in a bay. He turned to face her.

'Years ago, when I was as down as it was possible to be, at the lowest ebb in both my personal and professional life, Dick Drummond put himself forward, and at considerable risk to his own growing reputation, took a chance on me. But for him, I'd still be at the bottom of the heap. What I'm doing now is out of respect and admiration. The debt I owe him, I could never repay in a million years!'

Crystal was struck silent, shaken by the emotion in the voice of the man she'd considered made of pure granite!

After their goodbyes, Crystal and Dan watched the plane taxi across the runway, pause, then begin its take off. They watched until it was a random dot of light in the darkened sky.

'He's away,' Crystal said and breathed a sigh of relief.

'Close thing. Neville had to smuggle Sir Richard out of a side entrance at the hospital. Dick's nurse wasn't best pleased, but all the reporters were clamouring round the front entrance.'

'I hope he'll be all right.'

'There's a doctor waiting at the other end. He'll be checked out, and Helen will be there to meet him. Come on, I promised you dinner.'

'Where?'

'At my place. It's time I showed off

my culinary skills.'

Dan's house was not far from her uncle's. It was a lot smaller but everything about it was discreetly expensive. Crystal felt very grubby in her work clothes.

'I can find you a house-robe if you'd feel more comfortable.'

'No, I'll be fine, thanks. Can I help?'

'Mostly done. I left instructions with my housekeeper. She's off tonight.'

'What about Alicia?'

'Alicia? What's she got to do with it?'

Crystal blushed. He made her feel like a naïve schoolgirl sometimes.

'I just . . . er . . . thought . . . '

'Crystal, I'm just cooking you dinner and besides, Alicia and I have a very open relationship.'

Her blush deepened, and she wished she was at home. The whole evening was a strange mixture. Her unease persisted, although Dan was a charming and attentive host, and the meal was excellent, yet Crystal couldn't get rid of the feeling she was being entertained only as part of a debt! While they were having coffee, the phone rang.

Dan took it out of the room, but before he closed the door, Crystal heard him say, 'Alicia! No, I told you, not tonight. I'll ring you.'

Crystal longed to go home, longed to stay. Her emotions were in turmoil. At ten o'clock, Dan got to his feet. She almost felt his relief.

'I'll call a taxi to take you home. I've drunk too much wine to drive, and I've a heavy day tomorrow.'

He gave the merest touch of his lips on her cheek as he saw her out, and she was hardly in the cab before the front door slammed. Crystal sat back, oppression stealing over her. That spark of passion between them the other day, it must have been pure imagination on her part.

She tried to shake off the gloomy feeling of foreboding as she let herself into her flat. Just before she shut the door, the door opposite opened. She knew the girl, Kirsty, vaguely, in a neighbourly sort of way.

'Hi, Crystal. I heard your door. This came for you. The man wanted a signature, as it's special recorded delivery. I don't think he should've left it with me really. I hope it's OK. I signed anyway.'

'It's probably just . . . er . . . some papers. See you sometime.'

'Yes. We must have coffee.'

Crystal leaned weakly against the front door, holding the manila envelope with the U.S. stamps — air mail, recorded delivery. As if the day hadn't had enough drama in it, it had to end like this. Grimly she took the envelope into the kitchen, made a pot of strong black coffee, and slowly tore it open . . .

9

The print danced before Crystal's eyes — legal jargon, screeds of it, but the message was clear. It was what she'd feared and dreaded ever since that first letter from Dwight, warning and threatening her this would probably happen. In a way it was a relief. At least the sword had finally fallen, after months of suspended anxiety.

Yet, in those last weeks before Drummond's had begun to fall apart, she'd hoped that maybe the consequences of events in Nevada, by some miracle, had been avoided. Before she absorbed the full import of the two letters, the phone rang. It was her mother.

'Crystal? It's me. Dick's arrived safely. No problems. He's resting at a friend's before we take him to the villa first thing in the morning. I must say your friend, Dan, arranged everything beautifully. Dick doesn't know a thing about Drummond's, and no-one knows he's here. Crystal? Are you there?'

'Yes.' She tried to sound normal.

'What is it? Something's wrong. What's happened?'

'I'm fine, really. I just got in, that's all. I'm glad Uncle Dick's all right, and Dad?'

'All's well here, but I'm worried about you. You sound . . . '

'Mum, I'm all right, really. A bit tired. I'll ring you at the villa tomorrow.'

She rang off. Another second and she'd have blurted out the truth. They'd have to know eventually. There was no way of keeping this out of the papers. The Press would have a field day now and to whoever was conspiring against Drummond's, it'd be a gift from heaven — the final nail in the coffin.

She picked up the letters from the States again. It was hard to take in, but certain phrases jumped out at her

. . . professional negligence, court hearing, compensation claims outstanding, and the threat of extradition proceedings if she chose not to appear voluntarily. Her worst nightmare was turning to reality!

What hurt most was the curt note from Dwight Rogers advising her to comply with what amounted to a summons, and come and face the music. No regrets, no explanations. How could he? Had she really loved the man? At the time she'd thought so, he'd been so charming.

Maybe, after a good night's sleep, things would look better in the morning. Shivering, although it was a warm night, she turned on the electric blanket, had a hot shower, made a cup of hot chocolate and hid under the bed clothes, hoping vainly the dark clouds hanging over her would go away.

She slept uneasily, and woke to the telephone ringing. Blinking in alarm, she saw it was only four o'clock! She picked up the phone, trying to shake off

161

the feeling of dread.

'Hi, there, Crystal. It's Tim. How are you?'

'Tim,' she croaked, 'it's four in the morning! What's wrong?'

'Gee, I'm sorry! Never could work out the timing right. It's afternoon here. D'you want me to ring later?'

'No, I'm awake now. Tell me . . .'

Bound to be bad news, yet Tim sounded fiendishly cheerful.

'It's great news, for me anyway. I got married yesterday. Carey, a New Zealand girl. You'll love her. I'm coming home, bringing her over to London in a couple of days. Thing is, Crystal, if it's OK, I'd like my flat back.'

'Oh, sure.'

'You can stay, too. There's plenty of room.'

'Wouldn't dream of it. I'll move out tomorrow. It's been fabulous. Tim. I envy you.'

'Well, it's been great to have a flat sitter, and we're having a party as soon as we've settled in. You've just got to meet Carey.'

'Look forward to it. I'll leave the keys with the porter.'

'OK, see you soon, and sorry about the hour,' Tim apologised again.

Crystal propped herself up against the headboard. It was time to get a grip of things. Her friend, Tim, wanted his flat back — that had been on the cards for some time, though she'd hoped for another couple of weeks here.

She had friends in London she could stay with, or when Neville came back from Spain, she could stay at Uncle Dick's until she had to go to the States, but it would be better to play down her Drummond connection, though she doubted that would be possible once the media got hold of her story.

What she really needed was a good lawyer who was conversant with U.S. law. Uncle Dick would know one, but he was in Spain, and she couldn't involve him now anyway. Dan Farraday? He'd be sure to know the best lawyer, but the last thing she wanted was to let him know what a totally stupid and gullible idiot she'd been.

In any case, it could be the end of her career, the end of her life probably. Yet the slur wouldn't just be on her character. It would be on Drummond's, too. Right then, she made a decision. She needed help, and for Drummond's sake she must swallow her pride. There was no other way. And if she had to move out of the flat, she'd better get on and tidy the place up, five in the morning or not! It would be a way of passing the time until she could phone Dan.

By seven o'clock, the place was spick and span, her cases packed. She'd decided to take temporary lodgings near Brinscombe Manor. At least it would save travelling time. At seven-fifteen, she phoned Dan's home number. It was still early, but she had to catch him before he left. The answer-phone informed her Dan Farraday was unavailable. Perhaps he switched the phones off at night. So she tried half an hour later, but it was the same message.

At quarter past eight, aware she was going to be late for work, she phoned Farraday and Winch. She knew Vincent made an early start to avoid the commuter rush.

'Vincent, I've got to get hold of Dan, urgently. I've phoned his house, but all I get is an answerphone. Do you know where he is today?'

'Sure. He left a message here. He was in early. He's gone to Europe, Frankfurt, I think. I'm not sure what for or for how long. He was kind of vague, for him. Can I help?'

'No. No, thanks Vincent.'

'Crystal, can we meet?' but she had hung up.

Crystal's head was spinning. She hadn't realised how much she'd been counting on Dan, though when she did get through, what on earth could he do? As Dwight had so kindly pointed out, she'd just have to go to America and face the music.

She buried her head in her hands. Even the prospect of going to work was suddenly unbearable. How could she possibly keep her mind on her job? She heard mail plop through the letterbox. It wasn't a normal delivery but a plain envelope with her name on it. Puzzled, she ripped it open. Her heart jumped when she saw Dan's writing. He must have been here!

She rushed back into the flat to the sitting-room window overlooking the street, to see the familiar red Porsche outside. She flew to the lift, punched the button. Both arrows showed down. She couldn't wait, ran to the stairs, down three at a time! She reached the street just as the red car drew away.

'Dan!' she yelled, running along the pavement.

'Dan!' she called again, waving her arms frantically, but the car rolled away, gathering speed. She kept running. There was a set of traffic lights at the end of the street. If only they were at red. She took a chance, leaped into the traffic, and caught up with the stationary Porsche. She banged on the window.

'Dan, please! Stop.'

The light was green again, but he'd seen her. He leaned over and opened the passenger door.

'Get in! I can't stop here.'

'I'm sorry. I had to see you.'

'I've left a note. I thought you would have left for work.'

He looked at her distraught face, and then glanced at his watch.

'I haven't much time. I have to be at the airport. I'll drive round the block, back to your flat. Why aren't you in Brinscombe?'

'Dan, I'm in trouble. I wondered if you knew a good lawyer.'

'What kind of trouble?'

'Awful, in America. It could mean prison.'

He was silent for a moment, then said, 'You'll have to tell me about it. I'll catch a later plane.'

'I can't. Just give me the name of a good lawyer.'

'You don't imagine I'm going to leave it like that! You'd better phone the site. Tell them you won't be in this morning.'

Back at the flat, Dan made coffee.

'Have you eaten?' he asked.

She shook her head. Food was the last thing she'd been thinking of! He made some toast, and insisted she ate it.

'Moving out?'

He indicated the bags in the hall.

'My friend, Tim. I'm flat-sitting for him while he's in New Zealand. He's got married — coming back.'

'So, not a rich partner, after all, eh?'

'Hardly. Tim's just a very good, very rich friend. He's in the money markets,' she added irrelevantly.

'Where will you go now?'

'I thought bed and breakfast perhaps, near Brinscombe.'

'Sounds dreary. You can have my

house. House-sit while I'm away. No arguments, Crystal. You can feed the cats.'

'I didn't see any cats, and you've got a housekeeper.'

'Only a daily.'

He practically fed her the toast, poured a second cup of coffee, then sat back.

'Well? What's the trouble that's so awful I've had to postpone my flight?'

She handed him the letters from America. He read them, and then frowned.

'This Dwight character sounds a bundle of fun. As to the rest — I don't understand. A threat to sue you for professional negligence. On what grounds? What evidence? What did you do wrong?'

She hung her head. Tears weren't far off.

'Crystal!' Dan's voice was sharp. 'Don't do that. Don't go soft on me! Tell me exactly what happened, or I can't help you.'

She pulled herself together, taking a deep breath.

'I didn't mean to involve you, but if this gets out, it's Drummond's who'll suffer more than me.'

'Too right. Just start at the beginning.'

'A year ago, I was in America. I'd been there two years, sent from Broomhills Building to gain experience on the design and construction of leisure and residential complexes. I loved it out there. I worked for Rogers Parkinson. You may have heard of them.'

'Mmm. I know Parkinson. Medium-sized outfit, based in Nevada, with an office in New York.'

'Yes, but they're very keen to expand into the big league. I met Dwight Rogers, the boss's son, at a conference in Las Vegas. He was very attractive, charming, and, I thought to begin with, a first-class architect. I was wrong on all counts about Dwight but . . . '

She paused, reliving the pain, yet

wondering again, as she had so many times, how she could possibly not have seen through his easy charm.

'You fell for him?' Dan prompted her.

'Heavily and stupidly. He began to take me out, and we had a good time. I was, I suppose, dazzled by the massive house, swimming pool, sunshine! Dwight talked of coming back to England with me, going to meet my parents in Spain. It was all too good to be true. Then it happened. Business and pleasure, they never mix, do they?'

'I agree with that,' Dan said sombrely. 'Go on.'

'I was working with Dwight on a new project, a high-rise, luxury block, on a downtown site where some old buildings had been demolished. It was on that job that I found Dwight wasn't quite the white knight in shining armour I thought he was. First, I found he was working on a scam with the contractors — short measure, inferior materials, fictitious employees, you know the sort of thing. He was cheating his own company, Dan!

'The company was in his name, well, his father's name. Even then, I was still dazzled. Common practice everywhere in the States, he said. Nothing to get worked up about, he said and suggested we fly to San Francisco for the weekend. Maybe I already had doubts, but I was determined to enjoy my last few weeks in the sunshine state. I suppose — I wanted to believe him. It was the easy option. We went to California, and that's when Dwight's nearly-finished apartment block collapsed.'

'Not occupied, I hope.'

'No, but unfortunately it was next door to a hospital, and it fell on to that building. There were some injuries. I never knew quite how many until later.'

'But I don't see how you were involved.'

'That's the whole point,' Crystal cried out. 'I was so . . . so stupid. Dwight persuaded me it would be bad

172

for me to be implicated. It was best for me to fly straight back to England from California. I believed him and played exactly into his hands. He said it would blow over.'

'I still don't see . . . '

'When I got back to England, there was a letter from Rogers Parkinson accusing me of negligence. A report on the accident had discovered inferior concrete, cheap substitute materials, cost cutting enough to render the whole building unsafe. It was a complete shambles, but it was my signature on the order sheets. It looked as though I'd authorised those materials. Dwight had simply seized the opportunity to make me the scapegoat for his own crooked dealings.'

'Your signature? But how? Had you signed the sheets?'

'Of course not! How could I have? I was only there as a sort of observer.'

'Did you know about the concrete, or anything else?'

'No. I wasn't concerned about that

aspect of the construction, but Dwight, and the site foreman, between them, forged my signature, in case of any comeback. They probably never dreamed it would be queried. Now it looks as though I was to blame for the building collapse.

'All the casualties' families, at the hospital, are suing Rogers Parkinson. And, to cover himself, Dwight wrote saying how much he regretted allowing me so much authority on the site. It's all lies, but how can I prove it? I wrote, phoned, but he never answered, and I've kept the whole thing to myself.'

'It all sounds pretty suspect to me. Why on earth didn't you find a lawyer straight away after the first letter?'

'The compensation cases are only now coming up. I suppose I thought it couldn't possibly happen. I hadn't done anything, except act like a fool! It's like a hugely horrid bad dream, but it's no dream any more. I have to face that fact.'

Dan read through the letters again.

'I've been so stupid,' Crystal said, 'but I'm not a criminal. I'm so scared of American law, and going over there. And all the publicity — I work for Drummond's and the firm couldn't take another scandal. Dan, what am I going to do?'

'What you should have done in the first place as soon as you found out what was going on. Here.'

He scribbled a name and number on a piece of paper, and handed it to her.

'Mark Johnson's a first-class lawyer, knows the USA well, and is a good friend of mine. Tell him exactly what you've told me. I'll take these letters, and I'll send Mark photocopies from Frankfurt. And whatever you do, don't leave the country under any circumstances, not even if you get a summons. If you do, take it to Mark.'

He tapped the letter. 'These dates give you at least three months leeway. Do nothing until I get back, and don't be frightened into any action. Now that you've brought all this into the open,

I'll help you all I can.'

'Where can I contact you?'

'I actually told you in the note. I'm going to Frankfurt, where the Euro Consortium wanting Drummond's is based. I've discovered quite a number of things their directors ought to know about, if they don't already. After that, well, I may even go over to Nevada. I could always have a word or two with the Parkinson half of the partnership. As I remember, he was a pretty straight guy, although he seems to have bought himself a crooked partner.'

'Dan, I can't let you do this for me. I've been such a fool not telling anyone but I've been so scared — and ashamed.'

He took her hands and drew her to him.

'You asked for help, remember? I'm giving it, and as far as Drummond's is concerned, it's all part of the debt. If it's any consolation to you, I've been through something rather similar, a long time ago, but I still remember.'

Swiftly, he bent his head and kissed her. It was probably a kiss to blot out his own memories, but Crystal drew her own comfort from it, feeling his strength supporting her. She wished he wasn't going away. He kissed her again with growing passion, the passion that'd been there once before.

Crystal, at that moment, had to acknowledge what she'd known in her heart for weeks — she'd fallen in love with Dan Farraday, and it was all too late, too hopeless. He held her away from him, but his voice when he spoke was hoarse.

'We shouldn't forget, Crystal — business and pleasure never mix! And I shall miss the next plane if I don't go now.'

He detached a key from the bunch he'd thrown down on the table.

'Here's my house key. I haven't time to drive you there. Take your bags over now, and I'll call Mrs Weston from Heathrow just so she'll know you're not a burglar. Then get yourself back to

Brinscombe Manor. I'd rather pay out Drummond's for an early finish than the other way round!'

With a last brush of his lips against her cheek, he was gone. Crystal's heart went with him, but she felt he'd taken the whole burden from her shoulders, too.

10

Dan's housekeeper, Agnes Weston, accepted Crystal's arrival on the doorstep without question. She smiled a welcome which at once put Crystal at her ease.

Agnes established her in a beautifully-furnished guest room and promised to leave a hot meal in the oven for Crystal to come home from work to. Crystal made a token protest but secretly enjoyed the idea of being spoiled. She felt secure and safe. At Brinscombe Manor, she galvanised the work crew to a faster working pace in the following few days. She chivvied suppliers, dealt with recalcitrant contractors, and generally left Jim Reynolds reeling at the speed she lopped days off the finish date!

At night, she went home exhausted, fit only to flop in front of the television, eat one of Agnes's delicious suppers and browse amongst Dan's books and music. She had no desire to go out. Her life was suspended in limbo until Dan returned.

Her mother phoned regularly with news of Uncle Dick. He was now having a swim every day, was looking fit and tanned, and seemed well content to forget Drummond's meantime and leave it all to his son. Neville had dealt efficiently with the Spanish explosion business and squashed flat any question or rumour that Drummond's could be faulted for their safety procedures.

There had been storms and flash floods causing a land slip the day before the explosion, resulting in a natural cave-in. The actual explosion was another matter, and Neville confided to Crystal it was beginning to look like sabotage.

As the days went by and she heard nothing from Dan, her anxieties deepened. Mark Johnson, the solicitor, tried to reassure her.

'When Dan's got some news he'll surely contact us. I've had copies of the letters you had, and your own statement of events — not enough to go on without firm evidence. Trust Dan.'

Trust! Isn't that what she'd done with Dwight — trusted him? Now here she was trusting another man with her life and fate. Had she been a fool for a second time?

Her spirits were at their lowest ebb when she came home from Brinscombe Manor one evening, tired, frazzled by the day's problems, and with a painful shoulder which she seemed to have wrenched helping shift a load of heavy doors which had been delivered to the wrong part of the site.

A hot bath, a good long soak, and an early night looking for oblivion was what she needed! She noted the blinking flash of the answerphone, but there had been so many messages for Dan they almost filled a notebook. He seemed to have friends and contacts all over the globe. She hesitated, yawned, and decided a hot bath took priority over Dan's messages.

The scalding, foam-filled water eased her aching shoulder. She then put on liniment and felt marginally better. She couldn't be bothered to dress, so belting a towelling robe round her waist, she went downstairs.

Agnes had left a lasagne ready to reheat in the microwave, and a green salad. Crystal prepared a tray and carried it through to the sitting-room. Supper on a tray in front of the television — her only excitement! Then she remembered Dan's messages, pressed the play-back button, idly forking bits of salad into her mouth.

There were three messages — one, inviting Dan to a party next month, and another to cancel a game of squash planned for next week — all fairly routine. It was the third and final message which made her drop the pen and notepad. It was in a breathy, little-girl sort of voice. Alicia! This was personal! She should switch it off after the, 'Hi, Dan, it's Alicia.' But she couldn't.

She listened guiltily with an ever-growing feeling of despair. The breathy voice went on, 'Just got back from Madeira. Fabulous time, Dan. I must tell you, Dan! The news is I'm pregnant, and I don't know what to do. Please, help me. Call me . . . no . . . I can't stand waiting here. I'm coming round right now, so don't go out.'

The tape clicked off, Crystal stared in horror at the beastly machine.

Alicia pregnant! It had to be Dan's child! She'd known Alicia was his girlfriend. He'd hidden nothing, promised nothing. All the time and effort helping her was merely part of the repayment of the debt to her Uncle Dick. She had no right, and no cause, to expect anything more.

She had to get away, before Alicia came round. What time was the message? Quickly she hit the rewind, fast-forwarded the first messages, 'Hi, Dan, it's Alicia . . . ' She switched it off.

No time had been mentioned.

Crystal carried her tray back to the kitchen, raced upstairs, flung on jeans and a sweater, ran down again, her hair still damp. She grabbed coat, bag and keys, and went into the hall. She had no plan. Just drive around, perhaps go to see Neville, anything just so she wouldn't be around when Alicia turned up. As she got to the front door, a key turned in the lock, the door swung open, and there she was!

'Oh!' Alicia gasped, almost colliding with Crystal on the doorstep.

'Oh . . . er . . . sorry,' Crystal gasped. 'I was . . . just going. I'm afraid . . . I . . . er . . . '

Alicia stepped past her.

'Please, don't go on my account. I remember you from the birthday party. You're Crystal Tempest, Sir Richard Drummond's niece. How is he now?'

'Oh, fine. Much better, thanks. He's in Spain, with his sister — my mother.'

'That's nice. Sunshine and all. I've

184

just come back from Madeira. Is Dan in?'

She seemed quite nonplussed to see a strange woman on Dan's doorstep.

'No. He's away. I'm house-sitting until he comes back. Look . . . '

Alicia's face fell.

'When will he be back?'

'I don't know. I'm afraid I played back the messages on his answerphone. I should have switched yours off. I didn't realise it was . . . personal.'

Alicia smiled, reminding Crystal of a cat which had just lapped up a bowlful of cream.

'Oh, I don't mind. Everyone'll know soon enough. But I wanted to talk it over with Dan first. I don't know whether to be excited, or sort of sorry. Excited I think, if it works out.'

'I'm sure it will. I expect Dan'll be pleased. Most men seem to like the idea of fatherhood . . . '

She was babbling. It was ludicrous, standing there on Dan's doorstep, with Dan's lover, carrying Dan's child! It was exceedingly painful, too!

'Well,' she said firmly, 'do you want to come in?'

'Not a lot of point if Dan's not here.' Alicia was watching Crystal curiously.

'Dan — fatherhood? I don't think he's quite ready for that yet.'

Alicia's laugh was light and tinkly.

'Goodness, it's not Dan's. What an idea!'

'Aren't you and he . . . ?' Crystal saw a patch of sunlight, 'I thought . . . '

'Gracious, I'm not Dan's type at all. He's just a very good friend. My boyfriend's Alex. He's sort of difficult, moody, but I love him so much, I'm learning to cope with it. Dan's been such a help. He knows Alex well, you see.

'Alex works on the oil rigs, and is away for long stretches. He likes Dan to look after me while he's away. That's all. I wanted to talk to Dan about the baby. Alex doesn't know and I'm not sure how he'll take it. I don't think he's

186

ready for fatherhood either but, it's happened, and that's that.'

'Oh, I'm sure, once he knows . . . '

Crystal was light-headed. Even the thought of the worst outcome in America faded into the background. It wasn't Dan's baby! Alicia was not his girlfriend!

'Why don't you come in and have coffee?' she said suddenly.

'No, I won't just now. Maybe another time, when Dan's back, and you can maybe meet Alex. Fancy you thinking . . . Dan and I . . . ' She giggled. 'I should think you're more his type. It's time he came out of mourning.'

'Mourning?'

'Don't you know? I never knew his fiancée. She was Canadian, but, tragically, she committed suicide. He's carried a torch for years. It was all a bit grim.'

'What happened?'

'Oh! I think Dan will tell you if he wants you to know.' She put out her hand. 'Nice to meet you, Crystal. Best of luck.'

'Thanks. Shall I leave your message on the machine?'

'Yes, and just tell Dan I'm jolly pleased about it, only Alex doesn't know yet! It's been quite a relief just talking to you about it.'

It was the first night for some time Crystal slept unplagued by nightmares. As she switched on the early-morning news, she felt a surge of her more normal optimism. Things had to get better. She was right! The top news item sent her coffee down the wrong way. She turned up the volume to be sure.

' ... Drummond's Construction Limited, bedevilled for months by rumours, setbacks, and allegations of mismanagement. Today the firm was totally cleared and vindicated by the discovery of a dirty tricks campaign by a Euro Consortium intent on a takeover bid. Since the discovery was made public, Drummond's shares have recovered on the stock market, and the acting head of Drummond's, Neville Drummond, confidently expects to fight off the unwelcome takeover.'

The item was followed by a brief interview with an extremely confident Neville, expressing delight that the dirty tricks had been revealed, praising Dan Farraday, the internationally renowned architect, whose persistent investigations had brought the villains to book.

The telephone interrupted the news feature.

With a click of annoyance, Crystal picked up the receiver, one ear still picking up Neville's confident assertions.

'Crystal?'

Her breath stopped.

'Dan! I've just heard on the news! The dirty tricks . . . '

'Oh, that — yes. Well and truly settled. Shouldn't be any more nonsense from that quarter.'

'Where are you?'

'New York. Head office of Roger Parkinson. It's about your problem I'm here. Pick me up at Heathrow. Seven thirty your time.'

'Dan?'

But the line was dead . . .

How Crystal got through that day she never could recall. She remembered nothing about the drive to work except for listening to the repeat news on her car radio, exactly as before, but sweeter music to her ears, especially now Dan was coming home. The atmosphere on site was joyous. Drummond's was vindicated, there was a clear way ahead. Jobs were secure!

Traffic was heavy around the airport in the evening but she just made it to the terminal as the screens announced the landing of the flight from New York — on time! Travelling first class, Dan was out almost immediately. His blue eyes scanned the barrier crowd, spotting her immediately.

'Good flight?' she asked, polite and formal, desperately trying to keep her voice under control.

'As good as can be expected. Flying's not my favourite occupation. Let's get out of here.'

With a sinking heart, she led him to where she'd parked the car. There was a remoteness about him which chilled her. She concentrated on the traffic and was glad when they arrived at his house.

'There are a lot of messages,' she ventured, 'and I can move out tonight, now you're back.'

'What's the point of that?' he growled. 'I've got to talk to you.'

'I thought . . . '

'Leave it, until I've had a shower and a drink. I might feel more human then.'

With a squeezing of the heart she saw how tired he looked.

'Mrs Weston's left supper, if you're hungry, and I can open a bottle of wine. I bought some specially, to thank you.'

She sounded hesitant. He was in a strange mood. Why couldn't he put her out of her misery? Had it all gone wrong with Rogers Parkinson? He poured himself a small whisky, scanned his messages, and whistled in surprise.

'Alicia — pregnant!'

He smiled for the first time since he'd arrived.

'Yes, I saw her. We talked a bit. I thought, at first, it was your baby . . . '

'Did you now? And what did she say to that?'

'Told me about her Alex, and that she wasn't your type. Dan, please, tell me what happened in the States.'

He drained his glass.

'Well, I got a huge contract for Farraday and Winch — a beauty! A retirement complex in Florida.'

'Congratulations, but Rogers . . . ?'

'First things first — shower. You get supper.'

When he came back he was much more relaxed, casual in trousers and sweatshirt.

'That's much better. Now, let's eat some real food. I'm fed up with fast food and airline plastic.'

'Dan, I'm sorry, but I can't eat a thing unless I know what happened. The prosecution — what's to happen?'

'Oh, that!'

He touched her cheek lightly.

'Well, it could be life imprisonment, maybe commuted to twenty years or so in jail — probably an open prison, so it shouldn't be too bad. You'll be able to write a best seller about your experiences when you come out. So it should . . . '

He saw her face and took her hands.

'Crystal, don't look like that. I was joking. Can't you see?'

'It's OK, then?'

'All over, you silly girl. If only you'd gone to a good lawyer straight away, or told your uncle about it — not kept it all bottled up. Don't you see? It was only a try-on, and you fell for it. I couldn't believe it when I saw the so-called evidence, forged signatures, cover-ups.

'Your friend, Dwight Rogers, is one hell of a villain, nigh broke his poor dad's heart, and Sam Parkinson's dissolved the partnership, disgusted. He'd no idea what had been going on. He'd excepted Dwight's version of things as gospel truth. But make no mistake. Dwight and his crooked lawyers would have made mincemeat of you once they'd actually got you out there, friendless and without proper legal representation.

'It could've been tricky. You've been thoroughly conned and duped. Foolish you may be, but not criminal. You're safe, Crystal.'

The room spun. She would have fallen but for Dan's arms round her. Relief, so great it was like a release from a tidal dam, swept through her. She clung to Dan, shaking.

'Hey, calm down. It's over now. Forget it.'

'I . . . I can't ever forget it. I've been such an idiot — a complete and utter fool!'

'If it's any comfort, that . . . that Dwight is some operator. He'll wriggle out of responsibility somehow, but it's not your problem any more, and there's absolutely no scandal to be attached to Drummond's. That's the important thing.'

'You've cleared that up, too? Dan, how can we ever repay you?'

'I'll think of something.' He laughed. 'You can start by opening that wine and dishing up supper, if your hands'll stop shaking.'

Food and wine calmed her down, and as the truth seeped in she was able to listen to Dan's account of his exhausting trips to Europe and the States. She repeated to herself over and over, she was safe now. And Drummond's, too, was safe. She could hardly believe it.

'I must go to Spain, Dan, to see Uncle Dick, and to tell him everything.'

'I'll come with you,' Dan said unexpectedly. 'I'd like to see Dick. Next weekend suit you?'

'I think so, yes.'

The prospect of a weekend in Spain,

or anywhere with Dan, made her heart thump. She started to clear the dishes to conceal her pleasure.

'I'll bring coffee into the sitting-room.'

When she carried coffee in, Dan was stretched out full length on the sofa, eyes closed. Quietly, she put the coffee on a side table, poured out two cups, but when she turned round he was sitting up, watching her.

'Dan, I can't tell you enough . . . the relief . . . I'm so grateful. I don't know why you should have gone to so much trouble.'

He held out his hand.

'Come here and I'll tell you.'

She brought him coffee, sat within the circle of his free arm.

'What I'd really like to do is kiss you right now, but I guess I owe you an explanation.'

'Not if you don't want to. I owe you too much.'

'At least you should know one thing. You asked me why I hated women in the profession. There is a reason . . . a personal reason, other than dyed-in-the-wool chauvinism. It happened a long time ago, in Canada. I was there to gain international experience, and I fell in love with the boss's daughter.

'The boss disapproved most strongly. He had ambitions for his only child, Frederica. He'd desperately wanted a son to follow in his footsteps, even called her Fred. He was a Canadian Scot, self-made, ruthless. Frederica had been brought up to obey his every whim, and she allowed him to push her into the building industry.

'She qualified, just like you, but unlike you, she hated it. It was crazy, as she wasn't cut out for it at all. When I first saw you by that JCB, I thought, there's a survivor. If Erica'd been like that, she'd probably still be alive today.'

'What happened?'

'He pushed her too far. He was livid when he knew she wanted to marry, and saw to it I had the most difficult, most dangerous jobs on site. Erica began to make mistakes — a particular one I found out about just in time to prevent a bad accident. In the end the old man simply sacked me. I begged Erica to come with me to England, even bought her an airline ticket, but she never made it.

'The day after I left, she killed herself. Her family never even told me. I met her plane, and when she wasn't on it, presumed she'd changed her mind. It was weeks before I learned what had happened. They even denied me her funeral.'

'Dan, I'm desperately sorry.'

'It was a long time ago, but it left its mark. I never could reconcile to women in the construction industry, until I saw you. Your competence, your enthusiasm, your toughness were impressive — but for a while, you only brought back memories of poor Erica. You had all the qualities she'd needed . . . '

'I'm not that tough. It's a bit of an act — a survival ploy.'

'I know that now, but I was also

suspicious of you. I'd begun to wonder about all the mishaps at Drummond's. I thought perhaps you were part of the problem. There were spies and trouble-makers planted everywhere at Drummond's sites. If I'd known you were Dick Drummond's niece . . . '

'You would have disapproved even more.'

'Maybe, though I'll never hear a word against Dick. He's the only one who would take me on after Erica's father had me blacklisted throughout the industry. He even loaned me the money to buy into Farraday and Winch. I'll never forget that.'

'You've repaid that debt several times over. You've rescued Drummond's, and me. The debt's cleared.'

He stroked her hair, drew her closer.

'I don't think you were ever part of that debt, not really. I might have tried to kid myself but, even when I first saw you taking off your oilskins, spitting mad amongst all that rain and mud, shaking out your lovely hair, acting a man, yet so obviously, wonderfully, desirably, all female!'

He kissed her sweetly and softly.

'Ever since that day, Crystal Tempest, I've been in love with you. It just took me a while to admit it. I had to rescue you because I couldn't possibly live my life with you locked up in an American prison. I would've had to break in to rescue you, and that might've been more difficult than putting the fear of God into Dwight Rogers and his associates.'

He kissed her again, and Crystal knew the passionate spark between them hadn't been in her imagination. It was truly there, part of her life for ever. Dan lifted his head to look into her eyes for the answer he wanted.

'I love you, Crystal. I want to marry you more than anything I've ever wanted. If I rescued you, it was purely for myself, because I couldn't live without you. You will marry me?'

'Of course, I will. I love you, Dan.'

She lifted her face to his, and in her

eyes he saw love enough to carry them both through eternity. He drew her closer into the circle of his protective arms, and Crystal's heart sang with happiness as they sealed their loving partnership in a passionate kiss.

THE END

PERTH AND KINROSS LIBRARIES

We do hope that you have enjoyed reading this large print book.

Did you know that all of our titles are available for purchase?

We publish a wide range of high quality large print books including:
Romances, Mysteries, Classics
General Fiction
Non Fiction and Westerns

Special interest titles available in large print are:
The Little Oxford Dictionary
Music Book, Song Book
Hymn Book, Service Book

Also available from us courtesy of Oxford University Press:
Young Readers' Dictionary
(large print edition)
Young Readers' Thesaurus
(large print edition)

For further information or a free brochure, please contact us at:
Ulverscroft Large Print Books Ltd.,
The Green, Bradgate Road, Anstey,
Leicester, LE7 7FU, England.
Tel: (00 44) 0116 236 4325
Fax: (00 44) 0116 234 0205